VILLAGE STORIES

2019

An Anthology of
Stories, Poems, and Memoirs

By

Members of the Publishing Club
Laguna Woods Village

Cover photo by Miranda McPhee of the 9-hole golf course.

ISBN-13: 978-1-951109-00-4
ISBN-10: 1-951109-00-7

Editing by Peggy Edwards, Bob Faw, Scott Galasso.
Formatting by Miranda McPhee.
Thanks to our team members for final proofing.
Published by The Abstract Press.

First Edition

Other Publishing Club publications:

Village Stories 2015
Village Stories 2016
Village Stories 2017
Village Stories 2018

Contents

Foreword

Twenty-nine Village authors publish their stories and poems in our fifth *Village Stories* anthology. You'll cherish them all, and when you feel compelled to read more by these authors, you'll find many of them in our past anthologies. These are the stories that make us who we are and join us as a Village.

Some of our authors prefer fiction, others revealing memoirs, some explore the cycles of life and love through poetry. A few will make you gasp with horror, but others will make you guffaw. Included are the mysterious, mystical, magical and musical. Whatever your taste, you'll find it here.

The truth is, each piece and every author is a precious part of our *Village Stories 2019*.

Peggy P Edwards
President and Founder
Publishing Club of Laguna Woods Village

Ghost Writer

By Jill Amadio

Many authors need a day job until our books earn enough royalties and renown to quit working for someone else. One day job that grew and grew into an almost full-blown career for me began with a ghostwriting stint. It also led to writing my own mystery series.

I first turned into several alternate personae when a magazine editor informed me that a reader was looking for a ghostwriter to churn out a business book.

"A whole book? Impossible," I said. "Too many words."

"Imagine each chapter as an article," she suggested. After she told me the average payment I could expect, I was hooked.

Since then, I've ghostwritten more than a dozen memoirs, autobiographies, and business books that required transforming myself into a U.S. ambassador, a Las Vegas croupier, a Texas oilman, a Las Vegas taxicab fleet owner, a motivational speaker, a triathlete, and sundry others. I also ghosted two true crimes. For two of the books I was promoted to co-author half-way though.

Eventually a friend referred Jonathan to me to ghostwrite a crime novel. It turned out during my initial visit to his Beverly Hills mansion that he had always wanted a book with his name on it to display "right here," he said, patting an enormous Italian marble coffee table. His dilemma was that he had no idea how to write. Reminded me of the time I was at an airport shop in Indonesia and picked up President Sukarno's biography, a heavy red leather hardcover akin to a family Bible only to find it full of blank pages (he was still living at the time).

Initially, Jonathan envisioned a family drama about a typical insurance scam of which his father had been a victim. A little tame, I said, and persuaded him we should add a couple of murders to spice up the story. He agreed and said the characters must include his parents, two brothers, six ex-wives, four mistresses, and three daughters. I told him, No, no, far too many. I would take three wives, two mistresses, and two daughters, all the while struggling to

8

explain to him that in the book, they'd be fictional and would not resemble the real people. He stopped complaining when I asked which of his family he'd like to be the killer.

Occasionally during the writing my client threw a spanner into the works such as calling from Belize or Paris and asking me to add even more murders to the mix now he'd got into the swing of things. Luckily, he was pleased with the various twists and turns, especially when I included thugs from a Bel Air branch of the Russian Mafia (honestly, it really exists) as part of the plot. I gave the murderer my great-grandfather's revered Scottish name for some inexplicable reason, honored Keats by sprinkling quotes throughout, and withheld adding Cornish cuss words although sorely tempted. Instead, I saved them for my mystery series that features a younger Miss Marple from Cornwall.

I enjoyed creating a fictional forensic accountant on someone else's generous dime and planned to develop the book into a series. I had grown fond of the sleuth but Jonathan owns copyright, so my brilliant idea died an early death.

An inveterate traveler on both business and pleasure, Jonathan was absent a lot. In fact, most of the time. He told me to basically just carry on, and he'd read the book after it was finished. As it turned out, he preferred me to read it aloud to him, which I did, leading to another unexpected part-time career in voice-over and narrating audiobooks.

Jonathan pronounced himself satisfied. But then he said his third daughter was going to be very upset that I'd left her out. He insisted on her inclusion. Fearing my final fee in jeopardy I had her join the Peace Corps in Chapter One and whisked her off to Somalia, never to be heard from again.

However, when it came time to querying agents Jonathan refused to spend longer than two weeks on the search and quickly self-published with an expensive hardcover publish-on-demand press. For which I was grateful, nevertheless. Even though I had to watch him signing my book, my bank balance was healthy,

We soon had a book signing at Dutton's. Jonathan was having a grand old time chatting to the two hundred or so friends and neighbors he'd invited to congratulate him. As his eyes kept darting to the door to see who was arriving, I just knew he was hoping for a Hollywood producer, a director or an actor who'd slap an option offer on the table within the next three days. He'd begun to like this author thing. I decided to phone a film producer friend and invite him over to put Jonathan out of his misery.

"Hi, Brandon, how about coming along to a book signing right now? It's not far from your place."

"Who's the author?"

"Oh, no one you know.".

"So why would I come?"

"Well, I wrote it."

"Why didn't you say it's your book signing?"

"It isn't."

He snorted and hung up.

Since then I have continued to ghostwrite books, present how-to workshops, and assist other writers in entering the field. In fact, Kelly James-Enger wrote a book on ghostwriting and spent weeks interviewing me. Happily, she credits me for each quote spread over five pages, and thanked me in the Acknowledgements.
I like helping someone realize their dream of creating a family history so that their descendants can learn of their heritage. The joy on their faces when they hold that published book in their hands almost matches my own.

Evolving

By Lydia Mascarin

A bang of life from whence we came
Forming and circling the force of earth
Stardust
casting light into deep waters
Where consciousness descends into the abyss
Only to transcend onto stairs of moonbeams
Weighted salted waves keep me afloat
As I climb the stairs to a world of abundant creativity
One step at a time
For we are all evolving

The Door Gunner

By Doug Sainsbury

May 1970
Cu Chi, 25th Infantry Division base camp
Republic of South Vietnam

On Monday, Lt. Col O'Brien called me into his office at 0800 hours. Although we were in the transition from the hot and dry season to the monsoon season (hot and wet), the humidity was stifling and the mosquitos buzzed incessantly. Small in stature, but high on courage and integrity, he sat at his desk reviewing a mountain of correspondence.

I reported and he waved me into a guest chair. He leaned back and rolled a wad of chewing tobacco from one side of his lower lip to the other, then spat into a Styrofoam cup. "After you finish editing my correspondence, we're gonna' take a ride to Cambodia. We moved C Battery across the border last night and I want you to take some photos and write a story about this operation." His Texas drawl coaxed the words out in slow rhythm. His writing skills did not match his logical and analytical talents. When he first arrived in country, I had served, among my other jobs, as the PIO (Public Information Officer = War Correspondent = reporter and photographer) and he quickly tabbed me to report daily to his office in the executive Quonset hut to review and edit all of his written correspondence, with the exception of certain top-secret documents.

"Yes, sir. How long will we be in Cambodia?"

"Well, the battery will stay there until we can prevent the NVA from moving troops and supplies down the Ho Chi Minh trail. I'll only stay until I'm comfortable the battery is dug in. Y'all, can write the stories and take the photos for a couple days and then catch a chopper back here."

"Looking forward to it, sir."

"Okay, here's what I wrote so far." He glanced at each document before handing it to me, but pulled one out and set it aside.

I took the stack he had given me, sat in a seat in the corner at a small table, and began reviewing and editing with a red pencil.

"Oh, sir, I forgot to ask what time we're leaving."

"I told the guys at the Blaster Pad (Helicopter Pad) to have my chopper ready at 1000 hours. Why do you ask, we have plenty of time?"

"Well, I just need a little time to pack a few things."

The colonel laughed. "Hell, Specialist, you ain't goin' to Hawaii."

Embarrassed, I recovered. "I know, sir, but clean socks, maybe a second set of fatigues, toothbrush."

"Okay, I get your point. How you comin' on the papers there?"

"Probably another thirty minutes, sir."

Colonel O'Brien laughed again, spat in the cup, and lit a cigar.

. . .

I met the colonel at the Blaster Pad shortly before 1000 hours with my M16 slung over my shoulder, and my camera strapped around my neck. I carried my duffle bag in one hand and a notebook in the other.

The pilot ignited the jet engine on the LOH (OH-6A; Light Observation Helicopter, also referred to as a LOACH and had no doors) as the colonel pulled his small frame into the seat next to the pilot while I hopped into one of the two back seats.

We took off and flew at a low altitude, then quickly soared to a higher level; the LOH was a small, but agile aircraft capable of flying directly toward the middle of a tree line and at the last second elevating almost straight up and over the trees, an exciting ride I had unexpectedly experienced a few times in the past.

We arrived at the firebase in Cambodia forty-five minutes later and touched down gently in a cloud of dust. The colonel jumped out and found the captain of our firing battery C.

An infantry company was busy building a large perimeter around our howitzers and the tents that had been erected for both infantry and artillery troops.

I wandered over to check in with my gun bunny friends to get the scoop on what we were going to do in this desolate place. They showed me to the tent where I would sleep and we broke for lunch – the food was always better out in the field than in the base camp.

...

In the afternoon I took photos of our guys firing their guns and interviewed some of them about the operation. I also interviewed our FO (forward observer) who was assigned to our battalion, but attached to the infantry when they went out on field patrols; he called coordinates back to our fire direction specialists who would run calculations on large field computers (modern in that day) and relay instructions to the gun bunnies who prepared the rounds, loaded them into the howitzers, and fired on command.

The next day was more of the same, but an eerie shroud of uneasiness and anticipation hung over the camp as we were one of the first American units to cross the border into Cambodia; an ambiguous environment.

On Wednesday, I asked our captain of battery C if there would be any choppers passing through our camp that might have room for me to hitch a ride back to Cu Chi. He checked the schedule and told me the only seat available was on a HUEY (UH-1H; a large helicopter used for combat assault for up to six heavily-armed troops, medical evacuation, resupply), and for VIP transport that would be carrying an infantry general. Riding on a general's chopper wasn't my idea of fun, but if it was my only choice to get back to base camp that day, I would have to take it. After lunch five HUEYs flying in formation, one in the center, two on either side, one in front and one behind, descended on our location. I was in the general's and his staff.

I noticed one of the two door gunners had jumped out of the general's chopper and lingered nearby.

I approached and introduced myself. His name was Jim. I asked if I could have a seat on the chopper to get back to Cu Chi and he said sure, but we would be making a few stops before Cu Chi. I was relieved because I didn't want to spend another day or six with nothing to do in Cambodia.

I engaged Jim in conversation, the usual stuff like where he was from and how long he had been in country. Jim was stocky like a linebacker, his short, reddish hair hung down over his eyes until he flipped it back with a quick jerk of his head. He stood about two inches lower than my six-foot-one-inch frame and his flak vest appeared to be three sizes too small for him. He hailed from Topeka, Kansas and enlisted after he blew out his knee during his senior year of high school football, which put a sudden halt to college recruiters calling.

He didn't initiate conversation and answered my questions with an adept economy of words. I thought he was stoic. This was his second tour with the Army in Vietnam; his first year was with the infantry. He had applied for a door gunner position, but was too far down the waiting list when his first tour ended. He re-upped and applied again on his second tour and after a few months his name had floated to the top of the list and he won a job on a HUEY that flew infantry troops into hot landing zones where the enemy fire sometimes was quite intense. His good record moved him up the grid to his present assignment on the general's chopper.

"Why did you want to be a door gunner, Jim?"

"It's not boring."

"Oh, I'm sorry, man. Did you find the infantry boring?"

"No, but it's not the same as this."

"How is this belter?"

"More control."

"But isn't the danger greater, you know, people shooting at you from the ground?"

It became evident he was annoyed with my interrogation. He lit a cigarette, turned, and started wiping down the barrel of his M60 machine gun hanging off the side of the chopper. "Hey, Jim, want to get some lunch?"

"Naw. I ate at our last stop."

I wandered over to the mess line, took my food and sat with the guys in our Survey Team with whom I had taken several field trips, and had become an honorary member of their team. I told the Survey guys about Jim and how strange he seemed.

Webster, the chief of the team shook his head while swatting at the ever-present mosquitos. "Many of the door gunners are like him."

"Why?"

"Some are thrill seekers, like to spray the M60 on enemy locations and nail as many as possible. Some of them keep score. Others have girl problems back in the world (home). And some have seen too many of their friends get killed over here."

"Man, I guess I'll never understand that mindset."

"Don't even try. I just worry about what happens to them when they rotate back home. This place and that job can really screw you up."

"Wow, I guess we're lucky to be doing what we do."

"Too many guys over here become thrill seekers to beat the boredom, but with the door gunners, it's five times worse."

I noticed the general walk toward the chopper, so I gathered up my things and headed over to where Jim stood.

"Where should I sit, Jim?"

"You can take the seat next to me."

I climbed in, the doors on the HUEY were locked in the open position, and Jim twisted into his seat half-way over the side of the chopper, pulled his helmet on, adjusted another flak vest he sat on for protection from enemy fire from the ground, and checked his machine gun. The other seats were occupied by the general and his staff. The two pilots ensured everyone was in and lifted off.

We flew for about twenty minutes back across the border into Vietnam and landed at an infantry field location. The general and his staff exited and walked into the camp. Jim leaped off the chopper, unraveled a long fishing line and rushed over to a large pond created by a B52 strike and dropped his line into the water. I stayed in my seat. When he noticed the general returning to the

16

HUEY, he wound his line around his hand, rushed to the chopper, and eased himself into his seat.

"You catch anything, Jim?"

"Naw."

"You didn't even have any bait on your line. How can you catch fish that way?'

"It's all in how you jiggle the line and hook. Sometimes I catch fish."

"Man, you must be good with that technique."

"I've had a lot of practice."

We lifted off and flew another thirty minutes south to a camp on the Vietnam side of the Cambodian border.

Again, Jim leaped out of the chopper and dropped his line and hook into a pond, the expression on his face almost euphoric as he gently worked the line. Then he rushed back to his seat as the general returned to the chopper. Jim's countenance morphed into trance-like, same as when he was at the gun before. I marveled at the quick transformation and wondered if those two diametrically opposed emotions reflected the depth of his life in Vietnam.

We continued to fly south for twenty minutes to another base further east, deeper into Vietnam. Jim's face was on fire with anticipation as he vaulted out of the chopper and ran to the nearest pond to fish. I considered going with him, but I didn't want to distract him from his euphoria. After five minutes he turned and dangled his line with a small fish at the end; it looked like a bluegill. He displayed it for my benefit. His smile stretched from one side of his face to the other. I gave him a thumbs up. He tossed the fish into the pond and fed his line slowly into the murky blue-green water again.

When the general returned in fifteen minutes, Jim ran to the chopper and squeezed into his seat just as the general finished fastening his seat belt. We lifted off and headed for Cu Chi.

After we landed at the Blaster Pad, I jumped out and extended a hand to Jim. I had to shout because the engine continued to roar as it wound down. "Glad to have met you, Jim."

He remained stoic and grasped my hand with a claw-like grip. "Yeah, me too," he said with a detached expression. He remained in his seat while several other passengers deplaned as the general slid out of his seat and made his way into the base camp.

I loaded up my gear on my shoulders and said to Jim, "Be safe."

The door gunner nodded.

I stopped near the cockpit and motioned to the co-pilot who leaned over while tipping his helmet up to expose his right ear. "Sir, what's the story with Jim; he seems distant, unhappy, except when he's fishing?"

"Word is one of his friends got killed a couple years ago. I guess this is his way of avenging the guy's death."

"Has he killed any VC or NVA?"

"Oh yeah." He pulled his helmet over his head.

As I walked toward my unit, I turned for one last look at this mysterious man.

The door gunner sat behind his M60 slowly, deliberately winding and rewinding the fishing line around his hand.

A Gathering of Friends

By William Scott Galasso

Three friends, two centuries of memory between them, gather at
one friend's house. One has traveled an hour, another cross-
country. They meet in small-town Ellenville, a bucolic burg in
Catskill country, part of the old Borscht Belt, where comedians got
their start and boxers once trained in their "sweet science."

> leaves lisp in wind
> an albino skunk peers
> from a cord of wood

The friends sip wine, the years having left one bald, one gray,
one in-between, all laughing at the changes time gave birth to.
Then each in turn recalls some incident that saucers eyes,
until bellies jiggle about who did what to whom and what
were they thinking, or not at the time, which could have been
yesterday, though decades have passed.

> seashell fossils
> in old stone walls,
> a raven's squawk

The sun arcs, moments linger, the friends marvel at wins, mourn
losses together, consider themselves fortunate. No jealousy, no
judgment hinders the narrative until too soon, the time arrives for
handshakes, hugs, a last wave Goodbye.

> afterglow
> the north star brightens
> and calls me home

Wounds That Never Heal Hurt Forever

By Jacqueline Jorgensen

My mother knew everything; whatever the question, she had an answer. But in the hills of Puerto Rico, during the 1940s, there were no newspapers, radios, or televisions. The world news never reached that forsaken part of the island. So how did my mother learn all that she claimed to know. I remember her saying to me: "Stop asking stupid questions. I told you a thousand times that children should speak only when the chickens pee." To this day, I remember the mad look in her eyes. Still, one day I followed a big black chicken up one hill and then another. That darn chicken scratched the ground and made the crazy cluck, cluck noise but she never peed. And I got a whipping for coming home wet and with mud up to my knees. I didn't say anything about the chicken but I went under the house to cry.

Sometime later, a crazy thought popped into my mind. My life would be better if I were a boy. But if I didn't ask my mother, even if she broke my teeth, I might never know if a change is possible. If I were a boy, I would be allowed to climb trees, and ride horses like my brothers did. I could not see what would go wrong for a girl to hang one leg on each side of the horse.

It was hard to ignore my mother's rules, because something always came up to cause concern, like the day my father said that the school at the top of the mountain was now open and teachers were looking for school-age children. Mama's eyes stretched wide open, "Well, the boys can go, but not the girls. Who ever heard of girls going to school? That's ridiculous!"

My mother knew that attending school was one of my dreams. So, at the risk of losing my teeth, I had to ask her another question. "Mama, what can a girl do to become a boy if she doesn't like being a girl?

"What in God's name makes you ask such stupid questions? Keep it up and one of these days I will have to break your teeth. The angry look on my mother's face kept me away for a few days, but I still needed to know, so I asked again, "Mama, do you know how a girl can become a boy?"

My mother slapped her forehead with both hands. "Look, I am going to tell you how to become a boy, and you better stop coming up with those crazy questions. Do you understand me?"

"I understand, no more questions".

"Okay", she said, "here is what you have to do. The next time you see a rainbow, follow it and piss on its head. And don't ever come back to me with stupid questions". She clenched her teeth and walked away.

I stood watching her, but my heart was dancing with joy. In Puerto Rico the rain came often, any time of day or night. So, the next day, the rain came early and when it stopped, I started walking towards a beautiful rainbow. I walked up one hill and down an another, sliding on the mud and stumbling on the rocks. The more I walked the farther the rainbow went, and it soon faded away. I felt disappointed, still a girl, and wet from head to toe. The spanking I got that day taught me not to believe everything I heard, and to enjoy being a girl.

Billings Collected; Billings Recollected

By Dennis Glauber

No, this is not a reminiscence of that city in Montana in which I have, in fact, never set foot. Rather, I am recollecting memories of the billing and collection for medical services as practiced in my days as an anesthesiologist in South Africa many years ago.

My partners and I practiced our art in various hospitals around the city. It was not a matter of undervaluing our services.... we certainly expected to be paid... but by and large our modus operandi for making that happen was far less aggressive, almost timid in comparison, than is the custom in the USA. This reticence possibly relates to the fact that at that time medicine was still regarded as a noble profession, and that undue emphasis on the financial aspects was somehow inappropriate. We were, after all, physicians and not Provider # such and such in something called the Health Care Industry.

Our practice was, after a polite interval, to send out an initial statement detailing the date and place of service, the name of the surgeon and the nature of the operation performed. In those days many procedures were quite commonly known by the names of the pioneers of that operation. So, for example, a modified radical mastectomy would be named on the statement as a Halsted; varicose vein ligations were shortened to Trendelenburgs and pelvic floor repairs were Marshall-Marchettis or Fothergills. We had to put a stop to that practice when too many checks would arrive made out to Dr. Halsted, Dr. Trendelenburg or Dr. Fothergill and on one occasion to Drs. Marshall and Marchetti!

A second statement would be sent a month later with the notation "Account Rendered". Only on the third statement would the word "Please" be added. Then, if still unpaid by the fourth month, there would be a polite "This account would appear to have been overlooked. Please remit." Thus, it would be a full five months before the threat of "UNLESS" was rendered. Quite a contrast to the streamlined, no-nonsense business of collecting one's just desserts which I learned on coming to America!

Another feature of medical practice in South Africa was that there was absolutely no way that one doctor would bill for services rendered to a colleague or his immediate family. This professional courtesy was always extended, despite the frequent arguments of many colleagues that they had insurance cover and would rather the bill be paid by the insurance than to have to go to the trouble and expense of buying a gift in appreciation. We would relent on condition that only the insurance amount would be accepted; nothing out of the colleague's pocket. Incidentally, by far the most frequent gift in these circumstances was a bottle of a certain brand of Single Malt Whisky, a tradition so ingrained that one of my partners contemplated marking the label on a bottle rather like a radioactive tracer, just to see how long it took for his bottle to come back to him!

There was another category of patients besides these "pro deo" patients who of course never received a billing statement. It was our custom to extend free services to a remarkably (and indeed ridiculously) wide spectrum of patients including dentists, nurses, physiotherapists and ministers of religion. But in these instances, a single statement of account was sent with the usual details of the service rendered plus a clear two-word message "NO CHARGE".

This worked perfectly in the old days of manual accounting. Now, our practice was one of the first to switch to computerization of our accounts system in the late 1960s or early 70s. You would assume that the task of transferring from primitive manual to sophisticated computerized accounting would be straightforward, but you would assume incorrectly. In Alexander Pope's words, to err is human, but it takes a computer to really...... Our computer glitch par excellence affected some of those one-time only NO CHARGE statements. Unbeknownst to us the computer began sending those increasingly pleading and then threatening statements every month all still marked NO CHARGE. Eventually, one patient came to the office, part amused and part angry, waving a sheaf of account statements and begging to be shown how to pay a NO CHARGE fee before being hauled off to court!

My partners and I also owned and operated a freestanding Outpatient Surgical Clinic. The Clinic had its own separate statements for services rendered, detailing the charges for the use of the operating room and for drugs and materials. But for a long time, we were not permitted to charge any fee for the use of the Recovery Room. Eventually the powers that be authorized a Recovery Room Fee— a mere pittance of a few dollars. At that time, we had just had a massive batch of statement forms printed prior to this new allowable fee. Rather than letting this supply go to waste, we authorized our office manager to order a rubber stamp marked "Recovery Room Fee". The minimal space available on the statement form led somebody in the office to shrink the size of the stamp to "Recovery Fee" omitting the word "Room". We realized this when one day a patient came to the office to pay her bill and with a twinkle in her eye teased us with, "You mean that if I hadn't recovered, I could have saved myself five dollars?"

Ah, those were the days!

Fear of Heights

By Peggy P Edwards

She had just been employed by Braniff as an airline stewardess – her dream come true. She was so excited about being hired, she forgot about her fear of heights.

She decided the best way to conquer her fear was by standing on the roof of a high rise. If she could lose her vertigo there, she told herself, *"I'll be able to fly joyfully."*

So up, up, up, higher and higher she climbed, dreading every moment, but reassuring herself at the same time – she was so anxious to succeed. *"After all, this was her dream job, what she had wanted to be most of her life. It seemed so exotic, so adventuresome, so what I am and want to be."*

When she stepped out onto the roof of the high rise, there stood a man. He looked so calm and confident. She felt she could confide in him. She introduced herself then told him about her mortal fear of heights.

"Oh," he said, "There's nothing to it. I'm in construction and often walk a plank between buildings. Start by walking to the edge and looking down. Don't worry about falling."

He instilled such confidence in her, she did what he told her to do.

As she stood there calming her fears, he pushed her...

The Tiny Brown Lump
By Michelle Cahill

I've always loved animals and began advocating for them in the 1990s at mid-life (if I live to be 100). I was a couple decades into my 40-year career at Disneyland where one of my favorite things to do was visit the horses backstage. There was one baby I wished I could take home.

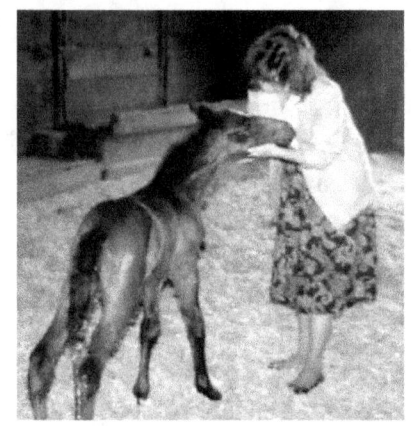

I remember being fascinated watching the ranch hands artfully braid ribbons into a horse's mane before its appearance in a ceremony at Sleeping Beauty Castle. Horse grooming and glam were new to me.

Having no pets of my own, I thought about volunteering with homeless animals and visited a progressive municipal shelter near my home. With a generous city budget, this four-acre facility provides all human, financial, and material resources for their furry guests' care and comfort. I began volunteering, mostly on weekends, and have now been there over 20 years.

One of my favorite memories is an adoption that happened very simply. Shelter pets often attended our shelter meetings. One such time, it was a litter of orphaned puppies—tiny four-week-old brown lumps, each small enough to hold in one hand. They were being fostered in our clinic, and our manager brought them to our meeting for us to enjoy. It was also a good way to advance the puppies' socialization skills and make them more comfortable with a variety of people—a key factor for adoption readiness.

I would often tell animal shelter stories at work and talked about these babies in a meeting the next morning. My good friend Donny said, "I want one." At first, I thought he was kidding, but he wasn't. He'd been wanting a puppy as a friend for his other small dog that he'd found stray a few months earlier.

Donny and his husband Michael came to the shelter, and I introduced them to our shelter manager who showed them the puppies. From this Muppets-themed litter, they picked Miss Piggy. Donny had cared for puppies before, was taught the specifics of fostering one so small, and given food and supplies.

They took Miss Piggy home to finish her fostering process. Once she gained sufficient weight to be spayed, Donny and Michael officially adopted her and gave her the much more fashionable name of Lola.

Lola is the only shelter pet I was able to enjoy from infancy throughout her life. When I would see her at Donny's house at her adult weight, about 20 pounds, it was fun to remember she was once that tiny brown lump I'd held in my hand.

Celestial Graffiti (1995)
By B.D. Faw

Some people need to be thought to be good,
while some are compelled to be bad.
Some of us hunger to be understood,
and others prefer to be sad.
But, I'll be content, when the last curtain falls
upon my terminal fling--
If it might be written on temporal walls,
"This one was interesting!"

The Pantomime of Pompey

By Lorraine Gow

My father's death was expected many years ago. What took him so long? I am now too old, too disillusioned, to behave as the one who would miss him the most – the grieving daughter: the one to write the kind last words. Our relationship at best was the thaw of winter; we never felt the drench of sun on our mutual paths. The man I called father, Ezekiel Pompey Wellington, became a man of few words – Mom, yes, God, country, love, hidden, revenge, 47 stab wounds, darkness – and as such he died saying nothing; the look on his face, however, spoke immensely – a sorry-ass smile painted where his thin lips were habitually pursed. His life as well was a misunderstanding of words: the stuttering from underpaid jobs, the impromptu excuses for affairs of which he was never at fault, the moans accompanying deep passions in which his forte in lying to women excelled. The animated lies are what I fell in love with, cuing me to betray what logic and common sense my mother had once told me I possessed in great quantity.

Pompey's lies grabbed me, spun me about like a falling gyrocopter, sent me into an abyss of no return – down, where up was not an option. Yet here I am, sitting at this second-hand oak desk his mama had given me, writing the eulogy for a man people called "Jive Talker." What do you say about the energy Pompey used in fooling himself? Maybe I should scat about the rhythm in his feet while skirting the truth – beep, beep do wa, do wa, bwi, bwi, ta, da, doop! Uh naw, no one could do it like Pompey: it came naturally to him. Just as on any given day, distress has become natural to me.

You know, I'm not sure if his life was a waste or a flash kickstart. How can a man live his life without yelling, without straightening crooked lines, without telling society it discriminated against men like himself because of their skin color, then turn around and tell me my path was crystal clear? Maybe crystal clear to him, but I sure as hell could not see the relevancy of my steps, although his epistles were there to keep me stepping. "Watch the man! Watch the man!" Where was I to go after such a pronouncement?

Like all men who considered themselves above reproach, Pompey would grab a word from his black bag of tricks – magic tricks – to fool his unsuspected minions into believing he was one of the ordinary people strolling on our planet earth. He was just out for a walk in the park to see the birds, to smile at the cute young things and to feed the geese on their journey elsewhere, but he needed a gun. A gun! Not any gun, but the Walther he removed from the dead, blue-eyed boy with the swastika, part of the waste he was ordered to pile-up and eventually buried. He had read some place that General Patton said, ". . . in war just as in loving you must keep on shoving or you'll never get your reward." Reward? His kind did not earn rewards, only the same refusal to sit at the counter or up front on the bus. It behooved Pompey, at age eighty-nine, to use the pistol on himself. A black man couldn't have shoveled wretched bodies into dark holes without feeling pride, pain and the rage of prejudice. It was war! That was his past (America's past), a past his night's sleep never relinquished, and his days never forgot.

Ah, Sweet Loretta never understood this precarious paradox of Pompey's life. She only noticed the grin on his face when she shook her shoulders and kicked her legs so high, hinting at the loose white panties she wore. Ah, Sweet Loretta never understood those night sweats were for the boys and men long gone, long dead in a war which settled nothing and only angered the returning black heroes. Heroes! Not even the President called them that. Ah, Sweet Loretta never understood the hurt that tore her man's stomach when his sex was compromised by love, money, and faces the color of warm condensed milk, like the faces that had ordered him to build, cook, and clean up the fiasco of America and her Allies. No, she never understood that, like she never understood Churchill. It was war after all.

Pompey, however, understood it all – lived it all. His rage ended Ah, Sweet Loretta's ignorance, but ended his freedom – if you could call it that – as well. It was the blade of his hunting knife which had lodged so deeply into the shapely bones of the woman he had only belatedly learned he had truly loved. With the progress of the Civil Rights Movement, the prison doors were opened, sending him adrift into colored platitudes tainted by those memories he shared with his soul. That's the day his words left him at the corner of 63rd. Street and Alameda Avenue. The jive talk was gone from his throat, like the clouded defense for segregation – poof! Gone.

"I can't be your sound; I can't mimic your history," I told him.

"You can be my son. My apology for . . . " Silence overshadowed his direction, his hands replacing his words: pointing here, pointing there, clasped together offering homage to the heavens, and finally, rapidly directing my life.

I played the piano much louder on that day. I drank more Chardonnay than a respectful church-goer would on that day. You see, Ezekiel Pompey Wellington forgot I was his eleven-year-old daughter standing at the prison door waiting to hear his explanation, his justification, his anger with the place to which I pledged allegiance, his laughter at the surprises in life, his "I'm sorry." I waited for Spring, only to see Winter cover my shoulders. It was no fun to be Daddy's Girl: I stumbled at cat calls, I wept at altars on wedding days, I ate too much. I have tried to categorize my father's shortcomings, his unhealed American scar. It's cold! And this is my reward for true love – writing a eulogy for a father trapped by an era. Clarifying the truth has been my light, although I have lived in the shadows of dark, silent caves.

I Choose to Sing – 1992

By Sunshine Lutey

I'm in control of what I do --
how I react to others, too
How I react to thoughts inside --
I'm in control, I will decide
Since music soothes my mind,
I choose to sing.

If I choose to count on others
and wait for life to start
In the biggest play called life,
I'll never get a part.
I'll take control, devise a plan;
if it fails, then plan again
Through it all, I choose to sing.

When I wake up I could groan,
drag myself from bed.
Could say I won't get up;
go back to sleep instead.
But I'll grab the chance to savor life;
got one more day to get it right --

It feels so good when I choose to sing.

Enjoy Your Cruise

By Jerry Schur

The Security Officer knocked on the door of the Captain's cabin.

"Come in," the Captain barked like a seal. "You said you had something important to tell me. Proceed."

"Sir, this morning a Mr. James Ankins reported to the Purser that his wife had disappeared. He stated that they both drank heavily last night, that they retired about 2200 hours and when he woke up this morning she was gone.

"I questioned the staff and she was nowhere to be found. We did find her wheelchair near the railing on G deck, about 200 feet from their cabin."

"Wheelchair?"

"Yes, she never left her cabin without it. I questioned the husband for almost an hour, but he steadfastly maintained that he knew nothing."

"The home office is going to hate this. Bad publicity. Terrible. Did she have an argument with another passenger or a crew member?"

"None that we could discover. Also, the maid and her table waiter believe that she was too frail to wheel herself that far, much less to climb over the rail."

"Did you find a suicide note?"

"It must have blown away when she went overboard."

"Bad news. What do you propose?"

"I'll phone public relations in the home office. A clear case of suicide."

The captain nodded. "Yes. Better than murder. Good job, Officer."

Two Gallons of Wine

By Cheryl and Phil Silverman

Two gallons of wine
Will make you feel fine
Three will make you shine

Never knew of the synergy of boysenberry
Of the taste of ménage à trois
Alcohol is quite benign
Anti-oxidant
With vitamin K
It's the kick of the grape in the vine

Two gallons of wine
Will make you feel fine
Three
Will make you shine

Fats Domino's Pool Party

In E, blues progression, fast shuffle
By Phil Silverman

Here comes Josephine
To my pool party in New Orleans
She brought along Shu Rah
With a barrel of rice and beans
At the Domino home
On Memorial Day
What a scene

My wife Rosemary
Made some crawfish just for you
I play the blues or any tune you tell me to
Here comes my old friend
Dave Bartholomew

Jump in the water the temperature is just right
Can't swim jump in the three-foot end all night
Parents don't let those children out of your sight!

An Epiphany
By Jon Perkins

Professor Emeritus Rudolph Greenstone taught advanced chemistry at MIT until his retirement. He believed that God had endowed him with a gift of insight and despite his advanced age of 78 possessed an active and inquiring mind. Once married to his childhood sweetheart, Rudy was a devoted husband until her demise from a virulent form of breast cancer some twenty years previously. His three children were grown and dispersed across the country pursuing their own careers and parenting. He seldom saw any of them.

His life in Cambridge, once a place of wondrous discovery, had paled with his retirement and subsequent inactivity. He became lethargic and fat, spending his time working crosswords. His contacts within the academic world couldn't be bothered to spend time with him.

Waking one morning with self-loathing at the condition in which he found himself, he made several promises to himself. He was once disciplined. Now he was not. So, he promised himself that henceforth his routine would change. Early to rise. Check. He sprang from bed in an old-man imitation of vitality. Brushing his teeth, he surveyed his red-rimmed, sagging eyes with pouchy bags beneath, wild eyebrows with long black curly hairs sprouting far from where they belonged. His red and yellow PJ top rose over a heap of flesh that was an embarrassing appendage. He would put himself on a strict diet.

No more crosswords. He had assigned a graduate thesis to an astute TA that focused on a problem he believed existed with the Periodic Table of Elements. His student was unable to determine the properties of an element that should occupy the space below Mercury on the Periodic Table. Daunted, the young man quit school and took a job as an investment broker. His interest also waned and now had become trashed in favor of inane puzzle games. It was time to resurrect his interest in the element Copernicium that had piqued him when it was discovered by Sigurd Hofmann in 1996. Classified as a transitional metal having 112 protons in its nucleus, it was an artificially created element that was short-lived and had unknown physical properties. It could not be determined whether it was a solid, a liquid, or a gas. What was particularly intriguing to Rudy was Copernicium's placement on the Periodic Table, just below Mercury.

Although the inferred properties of Copernicium were closer to Radon, a gas, than to Mercury, a liquid metal, Greenstone felt that an artificial isotope of Copernicium would share properties of both if a stable sample could be produced. He wondered what a gas/liquid would look like in the laboratory. Would it be ephemeral, like a snaky wisp, here one moment, there at another moment? Would it behave according to quantum mechanics? Would it help solve the conundrum of wave vs. particle? If so, could it be harnessed?

Rudy's partial insight demanded a finality, a grasp of the entire picture. Bathed in perplexity, his mind roved through a catalog of theory and presumptions. Sitting at his drop-leaf desk in a den cluttered with volumes and papers and scribblings and writings, he felt on the verge of an epiphany. His heart beat rapidly with a familiar infusion of adrenalin. One moment he was on the edge of a panic attack, the next a thought intruded and he sat back, his muscles relaxing, a smile curving his face.

How odd, he remarked to himself. What he was proposing in his mind was eerily similar to the behavior of an Unidentified Flying Object. A UFO. An alien spacecraft. He recalled videos filmed by pilots in the military and those flying commercially. Flitting here and there, UFOs were sometimes seen, sometimes not. Ephemeral. Sure, he was intrigued by UFOs, but not obsessed by them. Now he wanted to make certain that his imaginary Copernicium isotope wasn't being tainted by some needful irrational comparison. After some introspection, he agreed with himself that the properties of his supposed element were indeed similar to the ephemeral presence of an alien spacecraft.

An ancillary thought made him laugh outright. Copernicium. An element named after Copernicus, a renaissance mathematician and astronomer. How droll, the irony!

In his excitement, Rudolph Greenstone, an aging man who knew his time on earth was nearing its end, felt his heart skip a beat. Then another. Then a flip-flop. Then nothing.

Charles A. Black, The Man Behind Shirley Temple

By Joan A. Schumm

In 1960 on my first day at Ampex Corporation in Redwood City, California I was one of eight typists "clickety clacking" away on my "state of the art" Royal electric typewriter. We were stationed in the center of the room surrounded by the offices of the Purchasing Agent and the Buyers.

Suddenly everyone stopped typing. *What was going on?* I thought. It was so quiet. I turned around to see what was happening. Walking towards the Purchasing Agent's office was the most handsome man I had ever seen in person—Tall, dark eyes, clean shaven, smooth black hair and a smile that made you feel like a million dollars. Neatly attired in his dark suit and tie he nodded and smiled graciously to everyone he passed on the way to the Purchasing Agent's office. It was my first encounter with the executive, CHARLES BLACK, Shirley Temple Black's husband.

A few years later in 1965 with the birth of my third child, I decided I would stay home to care for our children. Yet, I loved the business world here in the San Francisco Peninsula and Santa Clara Valley where electronics companies were sprouting like mushrooms. It was a good time to open up a secretarial service in my home. I named it INSTANT GIRL FRIDAY! and put an Ad in the Yellow Pages.

One year into my business I had a dream… I wanted to have a unique customer to give some credibility to my home business. In my community there were three celebrities that lived within 10 miles of me--Tennessee Ernie Ford, Bing Crosby and Shirley Temple Black. I planned to send them a personal invitation to assist them with their typing needs.

A few months later, before I had a chance to send out my celebrity letters, I received a phone inquiry from a man who needed a speech typed by the next day. I agreed to do it and he would bring it to my home office. When he arrived and I opened the door, I was shocked. I enthusiastically said, "MR. BLACK!"

He was startled. "You know me?" he asked.

"Yes," I said. "I used to work at Ampex and would see you when you walked through the purchasing department."

We had a fun few minutes talking about the experience at Ampex. Then I found out I was typing a speech for SHIRLEY TEMPLE BLACK from her handwritten notes on a yellow pad. After that there would be many more speeches and decline letters over the next few years.

I saw Mrs. Black a few times as Mr. Black was my main contact. He would stay for a few minutes when he came to my house to deliver typing for me to do and brag about his wife's activities.

Charles Black was an amazing private man who had made many contributions to his country. He joined the Navy in 1941 as an intelligence officer in the Pacific and made more than 100 PT boat patrols—the same kind of patrol which President John F. Kennedy experienced. He also served as a scout behind enemy lines in Indonesia.

He was awarded many medals, including the Silver Star, one of the nation's highest for valor. During the Korean War, he was recalled to serve in naval intelligence in Washington, D.C. After the war, Mr. Black moved to Tahiti and, indulging his lifelong love of the sea, eventually sailed a small boat back to the United States over 7,000 miles of ocean. He also served as an executive at Stanford Research International and Ampex Corporation.

In 1950, while living in Hawaii, he met Shirley Temple at a cocktail party. When he met Shirley he didn't know she was a child movie star. He never went to the movies. He asked her, "What do you do? Are you a secretary?" Shirley told him she didn't even type. "I make films," she answered. "It was refreshing to me," she said, "a handsome guy who wasn't interested in Hollywood or anything about it."

Over the next few months, Mr. Black courted Miss Temple and they were eventually married at his parents' home on the Monterey Peninsula.

In the 1960s he gravitated to what would become the bulk of his life's work—aquaculture. Mr. Black co-founded a hatchery for oysters and abalone and later in 1966 created Mardela Corporation, headquartered in Burlingame, which conducted ventures such as catfish and salmon farming. Up until that time shipping fish hatcheries to other countries was difficult. Many fish would die while en route to long distance locations. Mr. Black wanted to help other countries raise fish hatcheries for their livelihood.

Then it happened in 1971 in Yugoslavia. After a 2-year program he and his team successfully introduced a new species to their pond farms, and constructed and operated a catfish hatchery. They delivered 21,000 yearly fingerlings and 110 four-year spawners.

This was the longest (10,000 miles), largest, and most successful shipment of fish anywhere. It was difficult to find news articles about this feat because Mr. Black didn't go public. Yet, he did tell his marine colleagues, leaders and dignitaries about it in his letter writing. *He had flown his fish to Yugoslavia and their people successfully set up a fish hatchery.* That was his message to the marine world.

I was typing letters for him to the King of Saudi Arabia and other countries as he shared his successful encounter to build his business overseas… Letters went to dignitaries and people he and Shirley knew--Cairo with Foreign Minister Riad and President Sadat, Lebanon, Italy, Sultan of Oman, East Africa, Libya, Zabreb, Yugoslavia, and many others. He was promoting his successful venture and Mrs. Black's diplomatic adventures.

In 1973 my children were older so I decided to close my home business. I wanted to get back into the corporate world that I loved. The business community had become known as *Silicon Valley* popularized by Don Hoefler in electronic articles he wrote in the weekly tabloid, *Electronic News*. I said my farewells and best wishes to my clients, and to Mr. and Mrs. Black who were getting ready to travel and move wherever Shirley's diplomatic jobs led her. Charles Alden Black died in 2005 at the age of 86 from complications of a bone marrow disease. He certainly had an adventurous and fulfilling life.

As Mr. Black said in September 1971, "My company just completed the longest, largest and most successful shipment of <u>live</u> fish in history."

I expect that he felt his "Fish Story" was one of the greatest achievements of his life, or was it the 55-year love affair he had with the love of his life, Shirley Temple Black?

Gratitude for Gaia

By William Scott Galasso

Life's a short song
a blink in Ursa Major's eye,
the pianissimo lap of neap tide
or the irresistible wave,

or a storm swelled stream
ballooning to river,
or an alpine peak
paper-cut sharp, scraping a cyan sky

until sunset reigns in fire, until
it dims to mauve, to end in darkness.

Treasure it all,
every green cliché of grassland,
every grain of barley,
every crystal bit of sand

and if clouds occasionally
make us melancholy or
rich brown earth muddies our shoes,

consider it the fare paid
for a planet's gift

until the stars we wish upon
call us home.

Haven't You Been Here?

By Mi Ja Park

"Haven't you been here?"

The sound of the driver's voice combined with the loud pelting of the pouring rain on the windshield made it difficult to hear, much less understand. We were also physically exhausted from many hours of travel, making this first encounter with a foreign language even more challenging. The cold March weather coupled with the pouring rain did not feel welcoming in any way. Our plane, arriving at midnight in a strange place, left us feeling anxious and even frightened to say the least. We had endured a very long journey up to this point: leaving our motherland to board a plane and after many, many restless hours, arriving on foreign soil. We were in a state of shock. Fortunately, in the midst of this, the driver's calming voice made us feel that we would safely cross the finish line of our journey.

In our entire lives, we had never flown on a plane much less traveled to a far-off land. Still, we had confidence that we could do it even though in the 1960's, foreign travel was rare. If it were a young woman, it was usually because she was an international student or a nurse on the Exchange Visitor Program. Even then, I remember, most of the nurses were headed to Germany. There were also overly qualified male college graduates sent there to do mining jobs, because they could not find jobs in the tough economic situation. They would work hard and sacrifice, and then send most of their income back to the homeland. Those funds were critically needed to rebuild the economy that had been devastated by the Korean War. Such sacrifice of these young men and women, who bravely seized these opportunities with their youthful ambition and fortitude for their motherland!

We, too, came across the Pacific Ocean to a place that was called "The Land of Opportunity." We were going to a dream country where traffic stopped both ways to allow pedestrians, even little children, to cross the street. A country that recognized the rights of the handicapped, that protected individual freedom and democracy, where honest work was rewarded and where opportunities were given equally. Leaving our parents, relatives and friends behind, we boarded, holding on to our pounding hearts, on Northwest Airlines which was the only airline that was operated between the two countries at the time. Bathed in a gentle rain, the plane started down the runway toward Japan. Perhaps, the tears from the broken hearts of those we loved turned into that gentle rain and accompanied us on our journey.

That same evening, an unimaginable tragedy unfolded. On March 5, 1966, a BOAC plane from London to Canada crashed into Mt. Fuji killing everyone aboard - a total of 124 people including pilots and crew members. The airport was sent into chaos and we were diverted from Tokyo and sent to Fukuoka Airport. The US Airforce emptied their compound and accommodated us that night. Early the next morning we flew back to Tokyo. When we arrived, we were offered a hotel room for our long layover. As we had slept very poorly the night before, there was nothing more enticing than the cozy bed, but we were too afraid that we would miss our flight if we gave in to temptation. We weren't even able to request a wake-up call, as we couldn't speak Japanese! Instead, we asked in our halted English. It felt strange to be speaking English, but we had to remind ourselves that was our new reality.

Reminded with the strange feeling of new reality we had felt in the hotel in Japan, we managed to catch a taxicab after we arrived in Philadelphia, the final airport. It took many hours to get there, nevertheless, we were there in USA at last! It was close to midnight. After getting in the taxicab, we managed to tell the driver, in a broken English, that we were going to the nurses' dormitory at the Albert Einstein Medical Center. After arriving at the hospital and driving for some time around many dark brick buildings the driver asked the question of haven't you been here in a calming voice. My friend, looking out at the streaming rain through the window, answered "Yes," but not without a little hesitation and mostly with a shrinking voice. After driving around and around, the driver asked again a second time, "Haven't you been here?" This time it was me who responded yes, a bit more convincingly and with more confidence.

It was getting later and darker and we could sense our driver's spirit draining as we seemed no closer to our destination. Finally, he asked a third time, wondering if he had perhaps not heard us correctly or waiting for us to speak more assertively. My friend shouted, "Yes!" in a voice of rupture that was held back from the time of our departure. A mixed bag of emotions along with the physical exhaustion finally exploded. At last, the driver sensed it and seemed to realize that we were having a miscommunication.

However, he quickly seemed to catch on why we were not reaching each other. It was not that we did not understand what he asked but, it was the language system that could have been at fault. The reason is that when someone asks in English, haven't you been here, then the answer is YES if you have been here, then NO if you haven't. In Korean, it is the exact opposite! Consequently, our problem was that we were answering in the Korean way, but he understood the opposite. This confusion made us go around and around in a circle, both in the car and in our conversation, without getting anywhere.

Once he realized there was a misunderstanding, the driver stopped working the wheel, pulled over, and went into a building. In the Emergency Room, he asked directions to where we were going. When he returned to the cab, he drove to the front of a building that we had already passed a couple of times. He went to the front door and rang the bell. After what seemed an eternity, but was probably only a few minutes, the outside lights of the building came on and an elderly lady, dressed in a night robe, slowly appeared, probably having just awoken from sleep. At last, we were able to take a deep breath - we had arrived! The driver helpfully pulled our two large suitcases and placed them inside the door and left quietly after collecting his fare.

We had paid $14 total, $7 from each of us. In these times, a seemingly paltry fare, but at that time, it felt enormous given that a whole month's rent at the dorm was $30. The total amount we were allowed to bring to this country and all that we had in our pockets was $30! Given his patience and service, we should have given him a gratuity, but it never crossed our minds because of cultural differences. He was a hard-working, middle-aged African American man who was committed to helping us and gave his best in his work. Although I can't remember his face, I remember him. I feel honored the way we were respected and thankful for his service.

Just as a beautiful rainbow appears after a storm, I saw the driver's face as a morning sun dawning after a night of anxiety and fear in a new land. Although our language, customs, skin color and appearance were different, I can still remember him anywhere, at any time. Although 53 years have passed, it still brings me laughter and warmth as if it were yesterday. His patience and kindness are stored together in my memories with hopes and fears of coming to this new land and embarking on my dreams.

I often wonder, since I first stepped onto this land, how many lives have I passed by? How have I been connected to them? Is there anything that they have imprinted in their memory because of something I might have done? On the other hand, there are many people who have touched me in a meaningful way. I feel a debt of gratitude to them that I can never repay. The dreams of my youth were facing and overcoming challenges, now my dream at this age is appreciating others. Appreciation revitalizes life! It moves our spirit igniting DNA switches for good. This is the reason that we need to seek for something to appreciate in every moment. Now isn't this the anti-aging secret that we all are looking for?

Spring Cleaning
By William Scott Galasso

Time to cut branches, dead head
flowers of bad intent, muck out
the brain, confine its detritus to
a compost pile, re-seed the mind
with fresh inspiration, let ideas
emerge as blossoms from buds

sweep out the spirit house
its webs of intrigue and rusty
reasoning, scour drab
despondency that shrouds
the soul's radiance, attain
a sylvan sheen, running
mustang free over green hills

forget past failures swallowed
by change, sorrows for which there's
no resolution, pack them up, drop them
in a dustbin, but remember lessons
ingrained, through pain, exult in love,
in the stuff worth keeping

and all those slights carried for years,
that make a question mark of shoulders,
drop the load already, stand up straight,
sing like a wren after rain

The Day Chris Came to Call

By Dennis Glauber

Anyone who has undertaken a major life upheaval, as we did in 1980 when we emigrated from South Africa to the United States, will concur that one of the stressful experiences is the process of culling what to take and what to leave behind. Books, artworks certainly, but also matters of sentimental value such as photo albums, theater and concert programs and accumulated magazines.

Two of the latter which definitely made the cut for me were the issue of TIME Magazine of December 15, 1967 autographed by the man on the cover and the South African Medical Journal of December 30, 1967, similarly autographed. The TIME cover story dealt with the first human heart transplant, performed by Dr. Chris Barnard and his team at Groote Schuur hospital In Cape Town, South Africa on December 3, 1967. The heart of a 24-year-old accident victim Denise Darvall was successfully transplanted into the ailing body of 54-year-old Louis Washkansky. What has become commonplace throughout the world today obscures the degree of excitement with which heart transplantation was received throughout the world more than 50 years ago. TIME was not alone in highlighting the awe-inspiring story of what seemed the ultimate, the close to impossible surgical miracle. And if worldwide coverage was the norm, imagine, if you will, the excitement in South Africa. After decades of (often but not always deserved) bad publicity, here was a South African achievement to show the country in a most favorable light.

How I came to have my copies signed by the "great man" is the topic of this story. That Barnard and I were both in the medical profession is irrelevant and purely coincidental. Cape Town is 1000 miles from Johannesburg where I practiced as an anesthesiologist, and there was no reason to expect that our paths would ever cross. I had been an active member of the young men's service organization known as Round Table. I had served in many capacities including the chairmanship of our local Round Table #3 in Johannesburg.

Having reached the cut off age of 40 earlier in 1967, I was no longer a member of the organization. It transpired that on a certain date in February 1968 my former club was sponsoring a gala screening of the movie CAMELOT as a fundraiser for the South African Heart Association. Somehow, they arranged for the attendance of Chris Barnard who would be passing through Johannesburg en route to a triumphant return to the United States where he had received his training in cardiac surgery. Louis Washkansky had lived only 18 days with his new heart, but Barnard's second patient Philip Blaiberg was by mid-February progressing well enough for Barnard to be able to leave Cape Town. (Dr. Blaiberg eventually survived for 19 months.) Having secured the presence of Barnard as the added attraction at the gala premiere, ticket prices skyrocketed and now I had my first contact with the project. I received a call asking whether as a fellow medical man I would like to host the distinguished visitor and his wife for one night.

We loved the idea and accepted with alacrity. Then came the logistics of the planned visit. I would meet the Barnards at the airport, bring them home for an early dinner before the four of us headed downtown for the big event. The next order of business, once we had told the children of the possibility that Chris Barnard would be staying with us overnight, was to emphasize to them that it was only a possibility that would become more likely with each passing day. There was always a chance that the condition of the patient might dictate a cancelation of the entire trip. So, kids, you'll just have to do the near-impossible and refrain from telling your friends and classmates. If the visit is canceled, you risk being mercilessly mocked and jeered at for making such an outrageous claim! Next was the question of where would the Barnards sleep? That's easy. They would have our bed, 13-year-old Harry would sleep at his friend's next door and we would move into Harry's room. The girls, 15 and 12, would not be disrupted. Nor would 4-year-old David. Simple.

The flight from Cape Town to Johannesburg took place as planned, but when I went to the airport, I was soon reminded that the words of the poet Robert Burns about the best laid plans of mice and men are still relevant. The Barnards had clearly had a mighty argument and the tension was palpable. With barely an acknowledgement of my presence she announced that she had absolutely no intention of coming to Johannesburg but would be taking a cab to nearby Pretoria and would stay overnight with her sister. Clearly this marriage was on the rocks, and indeed after their divorce, the then 47-year-old surgeon was married to a beautiful 19-year-old heiress. My guest was in pensive mood for most of the drive home but was cordial and genial on meeting my family. The high point of the brief visit was the photo sessions where he gladly posed with each child in turn, to their utter delight. He ruefully told us that he had better not return to our home after the premiere but would go by cab to Pretoria to try to make peace with his wife. So, on to the highly successful premiere, at which he escorted not Mrs. B but Mrs. G, and charmed the audience from the stage. We said farewell and assumed that that was our final contact.

All South Africa followed the news of Chris Barnard's return to his training ground in Minnesota and the veritable explosion of heart transplants being undertaken with varying success in various parts of the world. Several weeks had passed when my receptionist at the office called to say that someone pretending to be Chris Barnard was on the line for me. She and the rest of the staff were agog when I started chatting on a friendly first name basis with the real no-hoaxing Chris. He was briefly in Johannesburg en route to Cape Town and had a proposal he wanted to discuss with me. Could we meet at his hotel the next day? Mystified, and carrying my TIME and my SAMedical Journal for autographing, I set off for our meeting.

At that time, I had established quite a reputation on a very popular radio quiz show. One of several fields in which I had made myself expert was Classical Mythology, and this was the subject of his proposal. Barnard was already at work on his autobiography (published the following year as "One Life"), and would I be willing to write a chapter on the role of the heart in the mythology of different cultures? While greatly flattered and tempted, I gave it long consideration and concluded that I had neither the time nor the research resources (where was Google when you really needed it?) and reluctantly declined.

I had my two precious autographs and that really was the end of my brief tangential contact with the great and famous. Indeed, the only memorable family anecdote remaining from the event concerns our 4-year-old son. The day of the anticipated visit was a Tuesday, and on the preceding Sunday morning little David came to our bedroom as usual. Ruth was having her morning tea and reading the Sunday paper, but I had had a grueling night on call and was fast asleep under the bedclothes next to her. David took one look at the huddled hidden body, and remembering that the Barnards were to have our bedroom, asked innocently "Is Chris Barnard here already?"

Were Ruth's raised eyebrows and rolling eyes just amusement at the child's naïveté, or was there a tinge of "if only"?

 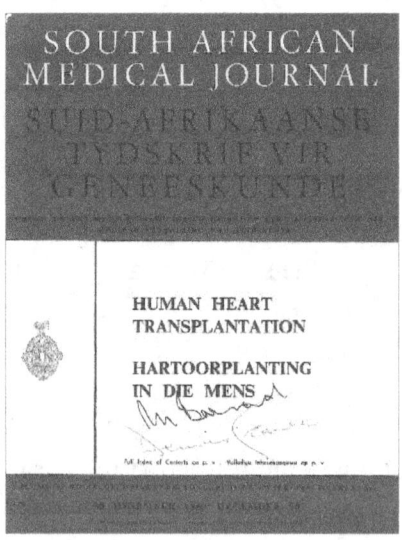

The Party Mind

By Ellyn Maybe

There are childhood parties where people play pin the tail on the
     donkey trying to complete the physiology of the animal.

There are parties every day where people play pin the logic on the
Universe. Whole countries get so drunk they can't find their car.

There are games of twister where natural disasters consist of
     people brought together only by chemistry,
      leaving their rocket scientist diplomas in a pile of dirty
      looks by the sink.

There are parties where the name tag is the only thing
     one is certain of
     doubt this
     doubt that
     cufflinks
     formal illusions required
     no casual banter
Just enough panic to go around twice.

Landline
By Allan Rankin

For a hundred years, the Twentieth Century was blessed by telephones. They were black plastic devices, sometimes in a variety of colors and at other times made of wood to look like a piece of furniture stuck on the wall, yet more valuable today than any. They had a bell, called a ringer not to be confused with a look-alike, but rarely seen anyway. And a transmitter with receiver, sometimes separate but usually in a handset mounted on a hook-switch. As the phone evolved it included a dial, and then pushbuttons in order to initiate connections to other telephones All by yourself, and, oh yeah, they always worked. Real people answered them.

They worked because they were connected to a landline, sometimes called land-line, fixed-line, main line, or phone line, but always real metal, usually copper. Simple! It was made to be simple because of the infrastructure and service provided by a telephone company. What a novel idea! These companies were usually called names like Bell, Central, United, General etc. Bell may have been part of AT&T, but you can forget about that. They provided long distance service—far too expensive. They had a monopoly, as did all the others to a lesser extent. It was better to write a letter and post it for a few cents.

Subscribers never bought telephones. That's right! They had to rent them from the telephone companies, who in many cases manufactured them as well. Such devices were far too complex for any Johnny-come-lately to be trusted to get it right. You rented them as part of the service, all for around five bucks, plus a little more to the affluent who needed extensions. Everyone was happy.

Towards the end of this great period a typhoon came along and blew everything away, or so it appeared. Overnight, everything was gone. The people woke up one day and everything had seemingly disappeared. Even AT&T took a hit and never recovered. This was not some whim of God or force of nature. It was technology. Perhaps it was the God of technology, or more likely the Gods, for soon there were many to meddle in all aspects of life and industry. The people ate of the forbidden fruit.

The Gods of technology introduced a new type of war. The wars were fought among themselves in fierce competition to replace the once-loved and near-sacred landline. Some of the people clung to their telephones, as if lifelines, tying them together. Telephones without landlines to hang onto, ended up in landfills. Many can still be found in museums. Copper was pulled out of houses and underground cables to be melted down for something more useful, like plumbing. No more Bell, General, or any of the other companies, either. It was as if everything had been vaporized by alien anti-phone lasers.

However, just as in spring after a long winter, drought, fire, or hurricane; new growth sprung forth. New entities like MCI, Sprint, WorldCom, SBC or TELUS, to mention a few, appeared. But they too were attacked by other invaders called Alternate Service Providers too numerous to mention. It has been open warfare ever since. They all disregarded the landlines, to use radio waves, satellites, coax and fiber, in lieu of copper. The telephone itself was replaced by things called Apples, Androids and Blackberries, causing much confusion.

The people struggled for years to cope with this ever-changing technology. Each lesser God promised much more for less money, captivating people with promises of enlightenment. All the accumulated knowledge of mankind was to be placed in the palm of their hands. Then, it became more invasive. As minds were won over, the offerings became more expensive. The people were persuaded they needed more, with games, news, sports, movies, television, internet, universities, languages and social platforms. The list went on. It was endless with ever increasing costs. They had been deceived, brainwashed, addicted, and financially stretched to the limit.

As time went on, some brave souls reported on the "brain drain" hypothesis, using the old-fashioned wood-based method of newspaper. Based on scientific research, they stated, *"Like slot machines, smartphones and apps are explicitly designed to trigger dopamine's release. Our phones' effects on cortisol are potentially even more alarming. Cortisol is our primary fight-or-flight hormone. Its release triggers physiological changes, such as spikes in blood pressure, heart rate and blood sugar that help us react to and survive acute physical threats, with the goal of making our devices difficult to put down. Mobile devices loaded with social media, email and news apps create a constant sense of obligation, generating unintended personal stress. Chronically elevated cortisol levels have been tied to an increased risk of serious health problems, including depression, obesity, metabolic syndrome, Type 2 diabetes, fertility issues, high blood pressure, heart attack, dementia and stroke."*

The same knowledge that the God, Gods, or aliens, gave us, was being used to forewarn the people. It went on to point out the good news: *"If we break this anxiety-driven cycle (average usage of four hours a day), we can reduce our cortisol levels. Unfortunately, devices are deliberately designed to discourage them (from breaking the cycle and reducing usage). But, if successful, it might actually lengthen our lives."* But it was too late. Technology had already won.

Among numerous mid-sentence-disconnects, power outages and worn out batteries, the people were helpless to resist. There were even viruses, hacking and misinformation to further confuse. Still, they craved more. It gave them power. They became divisive, often turning against each other. Insults, name calling, slurs and conspiracy theories became common among them.

Still, from the wilderness, a cry could be heard: "I want a landline!"

In response, a host of additional invaders arrived: Vonage, Ring Central, Ocama, Grasshpper, VoiPly, AXVOICE, and more. Each sounding more alien, as they continue to multiply. They brought innovative ways to defeat each other, captivating the people for their own purpose: Money. They claimed to be landline providers, but they rode on the back's other interlopers. Many shouted, "VOIP," as though justifying the deception.

"What next," the people asked, "Fairy dust?" The people wanted copper.

They wanted a real landline; something they could believe in and trust to be there in their time of need. They wanted something to connect them together again, instead of what pervaded. What they received instead was an app known as NAWL Another gift of technology spoken in ASCII, the language of their new God. Those who understood ASCII (American Standard Code for Information Exchange) were able to translate NAWL into their ancient and now tortured language.

It stood for, "Not Allowed to Want a Landline." They claimed if you text it fast enough, *notalowtawanalanline*, you would save money by limiting talk minutes. They lied! They wanted the people to pay more for the higher data rates of their own language.

The language of the Gods of Technology.

The people bought it.

The wars continued long into the Twenty-first Century.

To Dottie on Her 80th Birthday
By B.D. Faw

Octogenarian
means 80 years of age.
80 years of living,
with love on every page.
You had other loves before me,
who filled your life for years.
Some filled your heart with laughter
and some with pain and tears.

And yet that heart was empty,
the day that we first met.
You let me in to fill it, and
for that I'm in your debt.
For I, too, had a vacancy
where Love's supposed to live,
Till you came into my lonely life
with so much love to give.

And from this bond, a friendship grew
to fill our lonely lives.
No matter where our love shall go,
this friendship still survives.
So, call me Love and call me friend
and say that I'm Your Man,
And I shall cherish All You Are,
for I'm your biggest fan!

Character Assassination

By Miranda McPhee

The residents of Shepton, IL, population 7,657, thanked their lucky stars the day Terence Johnston moved into their sleepy town. He was sixty-seven years old, five foot eleven, and had warm brown eyes, with a few strands of graying hair combed cross-ways over his head to hide his baldness. He was a little short for his weight but carried it well. The town fell in love with this shy, unassuming, polite man who hailed originally from Crampton, OK. His arrival also gave the town's rumor mill a much-needed kickstart; the folk were friendly enough but just couldn't help gossiping.

"Mrs. Marsden says Terence spent thirty years working behind the scenes in the theater."

"He told my husband that he lost his wife last year and just wants to live quietly in a friendly town like ours."

"Miss Page at the Library told me Terence has been checking out books about real-life murder mysteries."

"Terence told my sister-in-law Lucy that he was a stage manager. He'd wanted to be an actor but it seemed he wasn't good enough. She said he looked so disappointed."

"I saw Terence buying outdoor gear the other day and some maps."

"Do you know what time the gardening center opens? Terence needs to buy a spade for his garden."

"I hear Terence needs to take in a lodger as he needs the income."

"Well, he won't have got rich working in the theater. Poor man, tsk."

After a month, the townsfolk settled down as there was little more to know. Terence was seen running personal errands around town but otherwise led a quiet life, preferring to keep his own company in the small, secluded house he bought on the edge of town. The rumor about needing to rent out a room proved to be true when he told the butcher, who duly passed the information around the town, that he had a lodger moving in, a Mrs. Vera Windalow. He said he didn't know much about her and hoped she would be ok, but beggars couldn't be choosers, as not many people wanted to live in a tiny house in a tiny town, let alone share a bathroom with an old guy like himself.

It didn't take long for things to start going wrong.

Vera Windalow was a cranky, ninety-something-year-old who appeared to have a grudge against the world. She was a slightly hunched woman who wore dull, loose-fitting clothes and shuffled along using a cane. From the day she arrived, she had a nasty habit of staring down people with her black, beady eyes. The townsfolk gave her the benefit of the doubt to begin with, hoping to charm her into a smile. Maybe she's had a life of disappointment and hardship that's turned her into a bitter old woman, they thought.

Wrong. It soon became apparent that Vera was just was a downright nasty woman. For everything the Shepton townsfolk loved about Terence Johnston, they loathed about his lodger. It wasn't so much that Vera didn't have a kind word to say about anyone; rather she went out of her way to spread misery and disgust all over the tiny town.

Mrs. Barrie first encountered Vera when she popped into the pharmacy to pick up some cough mixture. To her face, in front of her twins in their stroller, Vera said loudly, "I was in Cobbleton the other day, I saw your husband in the pharmacy. Why would your husband need to go to a pharmacy ten miles away? Buying Viagra again, is he? Got another woman, has he?" Mrs. Barrie fled. Dinner conversation at the Barries' house that night was simply awful.

Standing in line at the bank, Vera looked around for a victim and found the bank loan officer, Penelope Barker. "I see you've put on a lot of weight," she barked at the young woman. "Are you just eating too much or is it a nine-month thing? Do you know who the father is?" Penelope Barker, an unmarried woman who had indeed gained a pound or two, was horrified, but any reaction was stifled by her training never be rude to a customer. Word got to Penelope's boyfriend who panicked at the possibility of impending fatherhood, terrified it might be true.

Vera Windalow openly smacked her lips with satisfaction at the discomfort she caused. She cared not one jot whether her tongue lashings were pure fabrication. She quickly and inevitably found herself alone. Alone in the line at the pharmacy, the supermarket, the bank. The lines of people queuing for services on a busy Monday morning would vanish as soon as Vera shuffled in grumbling about everything in sight, looking for victims on whom to unleash her daily dose of vitriol. Even the gang of high-school bullies left her alone, in case the safety they found in numbers wasn't there one night and one of them faced her wrath alone. Nobody dared ask the old woman why she was this way. She didn't seem demented, just vicious, taking a perverse pride in the misery of others. Terence was as surprised and horrified as everyone else. Every single time he now went into town, someone accosted him, begging him to evict her.

"I'd like to but I can't," he kept saying. "She's a tenant and it seems tenants have more rights than ever these days. I'm sorry, she checked out ok; her nephew brought her and she barely said a word. He paid cash in advance, left her with some money, and said he'd be back at the end of the lease. He said they'd found her a retirement community to live in when space became available. There's really nothing I can do. But at least it's only for six months. I tried calling her nephew but Vera said his phone had been cut off as he didn't pay the bill."

There were five more months to go; the town would just have to put up with the woman. But it got worse and worse. Vera Windalow became a curtain-twitcher, peeking out from behind the living room curtain like a venomous frog on a lily pad, waiting for another passerby to berate. Heaving up the bottom sash window, she would fire off snide remarks like whale harpoons, cackling at the locals' discomfort and disgust. She never acted this way when Terence was home, so he never actually witnessed it, making it harder for him to crack the landlord's whip. He told his neighbor that she'd snarled "All hearsay and lies!" at him when he dared mention it.

She delighted in going into town every day, hellbent on finding a target. Worst of all, she seemed to enjoy it so much. She wasn't breaking any laws, so there was little the townsfolk could do other than avoid and ignore her. But every taunt sowed a seed of doubt about who was doing things they shouldn't. Vera was telling lies. Pure lies. *Wasn't* she? Or *was* she?

The pressure on Terence from the townsfolk became excruciating.

"It's really hard for me as I'm around so little," he said apologetically. I don't actually see her being nasty. I spend so much time hiking, and you know I don't come into town much. I'm so sorry." He was obviously devastated about what was going on but felt helpless.

The gossip turned nasty one morning.

"Vera Windalow needs her mouth washed out with soap."

"She'll get what's coming to her one of these days."

"Someone's going to take care of that woman, you mark my words."

"Jeez, I hope so, and soon."

Two days later, Vera Windalow disappeared. Her disappearance was marked by a decided *lack* of cringing, hiding round corners, peeping through store windows to see if it was safe to go inside. Vera was nowhere to be seen. Terence was away at his niece's wedding, and there were no lights on in his house.

"Maybe she's lying on the floor hurt or even dead," suggested the librarian, Laura Page, her natural kindness rising above her loathing. Nobody had a kind word to say in response, such was the ill will the old woman had sown. Nobody offered to go and look.

The gossip mill was silent. Everyone thought and perhaps even assumed that one or more of their own townsfolk had done away with Vera Windalow and buried her somewhere in the natural mountains around them, never to be found – in their lifetime anyway. Nobody wanted to start a conversation about it, nobody wanted to know, nobody dared rock the fragile boat. Some thought, hoped perhaps, that Terence had done her in. Good riddance.

Terence returned to town a few days later to find his tenant gone. All her belongings were still in her room – her dowdy clothes, creams, hairnets, even her cane, which was curious. She had very few personal effects other than toiletries. John Hodson, who had a triple role in town as the bank manager, sheriff, and chair of the PTA, went to Terence's house to have a look. It was true. Vera had, purely and simply, vanished.

At the PTA meeting the following night, John Hodson called the meeting to order, but education was the last thing on anyone's mind. The topic quickly turned to the missing Vera Windalow.

"Should we file a missing person's report?" asked Mrs. Lambert hesitantly.

"Why would we want to do that?" countered Mr. Barrie, whose wife still didn't know whether to believe he wasn't buying Viagra for another woman nor having an affair. "All those who'd rather Vera Windalow stayed missing, raise your hand." Every hand in the room shot up, the count was unanimous.

"Well," said John Hodson slowly, stroking his beard thoughtfully. "Maybe we don't have to do anything by law, if we don't consider it any of our business." There was a collective intake of breath.

"But what about Terence?" asked the librarian, Laura Page. All the heads swiveled back to the chairman, their eyes pleading for a good answer.

"Hmm," he said, "Well I guess that's a problem..."

"Wait! What if we paid him off?" demanded Mr. Higgs the butcher. "None of us are rich, but I'd give money to keep that ghastly woman off my doorstep." The room was quickly filled with cries of "Me too!" "Yes!" "Great idea!"

"Let's think this through," the loan officer piped up. "She didn't have a bank account here as she said she didn't trust anyone. And Terence once said she must be lonely as she never got mail or visitors. And we know that her nephew paid her rent for six months in advance and is uncontactable. So when her nephew comes to collect her, we'll just have to say we have no idea where she went. Or something..." she tailed off lamely.

The butcher rose to his feet. "Perfect! All those in favor, raise your hand," he called out, anxious to keep the momentum going behind his idea. Every hand shot up, again the count was unanimous.

And so it was. The dislike of Vera Windalow was so intense that the townsfolk collected almost two hundred thousand dollars to buy Terence Johnston's silence, raiding their coffers and IRAs in the name of peace and a coverup. Mr. Higgs the butcher made the deal with Terence so that Sheriff John Hodson could plead ignorance if he was ever asked. Terence would deal with Vera's nephew and rid his house of any sign of her, and life would go on. But Terence said he felt uncomfortable still living in the town when nobody knew what had happened to Vera; maybe the townsfolk would think it was his doing, even if he wasn't even here when she went missing. No, no, they reassured him, but not really sure at all. Terence had, after all, bought a spade, gone on hikes, and checked out murder mystery books from the library. Truth be told, they didn't want to know. So the town stretched deeper into its collective pockets and bought his house at the price he paid plus ten percent.

Terence left town with a suitcase full of cash and left no forwarding address. Shepton, IL, population 7,657, breathed a sigh of relief and went back to its sleepy ways. The townsfolk were a good deal poorer and the worse for wear, and bound together by the suspicion that one of them could be a murderer, or perhaps they had just paid one off. All was well, and it was as though Vera never existed.

Terence drove for eight hours through the night from Shepton, IL, to Crampton, OK. He pulled into the driveway of a large family home and parked, got his suitcase out of the trunk, took a key from his pocket, and let himself in the front door. He crept up the stairs and into the master bedroom. He bent over to kiss the woman sleeping in the bed, then perched on the side, watching as she opened her eyes sleepily.

"Hello, my love," he said, kissing his wife again.

"Hello darling, I'm so glad you're home at last. This job took *ages*!"

"Yes, I know, I'm sorry, but it was worth it."

His wife giggled. "Were you using Vera again?"

"Yup. She's one nasty piece of work, she never fails to make them pay up."

"Are you sure they won't talk?"

"Not a chance! They think I might be a murderer, so they couldn't wait to see the back of me."

"Did anyone suspect you were actually Vera?

"Nope, they were so busy dealing with all the nasty insinuations. Then they couldn't bury Vera fast enough. It's the same reaction every time I do this."

His wife laughed out loud. "You must be exhausted; come to bed."

It's true, he was exhausted after months in Shepton, IL. He may not have made it to the boards as an actor, but he'd spent three decades as a stage manager. He'd stood in the wings at rehearsal after rehearsal and studied actors creating their characters, using props, making lightning-fast changes between scenes, and improvising when things didn't go according to plan. He'd watched makeup artists transforming people into entirely new personae, copied choreographers creating new movements, and listened to voice coaches and directors. So he couldn't act, huh? Now he had top billing in the town of his choice with a character he'd invented. Tomorrow, he thought sleepily, he'd decide where he and his wonderful creation, Vera Windalow, would go next.

Streetheart

(Detroit, 1967)

By Cheryl and Phil Silverman

He looks cool on multi speed wheels
Riding too fast in the rain
Wonder just how that feels
Can it alleviate some psychic pain

(Be) Street smart
Street heart
My Mother told me
Be Street smart

Let see if he goes through that red light
Bikers break the rules
Might not be too bright
Or Mensa oh so cool!

(Be) Street smart
Sweet heart
My mother told me
Be Street smart

Sure he must own a Harley or a Honda
Both in the shop today
Tooling around town on his Schwinn makes me wonder
What he's really got to say

Afraid to pass Eight Mile
into Detroit
Ferndale is safer
Don't worry about getting hurt
One can walk unlike a waifer
Stay Street Smart little lady
Stay home and open a tome

(Be) Street smart
Sweetheart
My Mother said
Be Street smart

One Summer Afternoon With My Grandma the Spinner

By Daya Shankar

The year was 1945, my mother and I went to visit my grandma Devi who lived in a town named Bijnor that is situated just a few hundred miles North of Delhi, India. Bijnor is a small town surrounded by villages. The villagers depended mostly on agriculture. The soil was fertile and the irrigation was very good as the water would be supplied from the banks of the river Ganges.

Grandma Spinner had beautiful olive color skin. A shining golden tone would add a unique shimmer to her wrinkled but smiley face. Her silver colored hair was particularly beautiful when she would get it shampooed and sit under the morning Sun to dry it. She would braid her hair and wrap the braid in a circle and gently place it on the back of her head. Her soft light brown eyes were always filled with affection and love. Very attractive indeed. People would gravitate to my grandma almost instantly. Children would often call her "Devi Ma".

One of my grandma's favorite pastimes was - spinning, singing, and telling stories. The children from surrounding villages would come to watch her spin and listen to her songs and stories. Some of her stories were famous for their social and historical context. The spinning hour of my grandma became even more enjoyable when she would give the children her home-baked cookies with a glass of fresh homemade lemonade.

Tuesday was a particularly busy day for my grandma as more children would come to spinning hour. Because every Tuesday was a teacher's day and the school would not be in session. Along with all the participating children I too would look forward to every Tuesday afternoon. As a little girl I was amazed to see how my grandma was able to change a cotton ball into the fine long threads as she would keep spinning the wheel. The whole process to me was just magical!

One day a friend of mine named Shamu asked, "Devi Ma, why do you spin churkha--the spinning wheel?"

"It is a long story, do you really want to hear it?" said Devi Ma.

"Yes, we really want to hear, please tell us," said all the children in an insisting tone."

"Alright, I will. Our great leader Gandhi ji inspired me to learn to spin. It is because of Gandhiji that not just me but many people have begun to learn to spin."

"People also know him as Mahatma Gandhi. Mahatma means the Great Soul. Some of you perhaps have heard about him?" Several children raised hand and shouted, "Yes we have."

"Good. I am glad that you heard about him. He is our great leader who motivates us to see our inner strength. He teaches us the importance of being self-sufficient, self-reliant, independence, and freedom. He teaches us that it is our duty to develop our God-given talents, like learning to read and write, we should learn to make our own fabric. We can do that by learning to spin cotton. You see children if we can learn to spin cotton then weavers can make fabric out of the spun threads and the fabric can be used to sew our garments. You do not have to wait to buy the fabric from the British merchants who occupy your country and they also control the natural resources, raw material like cotton."

"Devi Ma, what do you mean when you say that he teaches us the importance of freedom - becoming free?"

"Well you see children, right now we are not free. We have to do whatever the British people order us to do, because they have occupied our country, they can order us and we have to do what they tell us to do.

"But why?" Well children you see many years ago, rather hundreds of years ago, some greedy British merchants came from England and tricked our leaders and the rulers. In the beginning they appeared to be trustworthy.

"What do you mean by trustworthy?" asked Kumkum.

"That means that you can believe them and that they seem to be telling the truth. But they were not. These merchants were known as East India Company. In beginning they made themselves look like they were good and honest but they were telling a lie and they were deceptive.

"They would take away all our natural resources the raw material like the cotton and they would send these to England. There they will use our raw material to make different type of products and tell the people in India that whatever was made in England was superior and things made in India are inferior. They would give strict orders, <u>do not buy anything that is made in India.</u>

"You see my dear ones this has been going on for a long time. People in India have no rights. They are deprived of even their basic rights. They are not allowed to learn any skills. They are forced to promote foreign goods and they would belittle anything that is made in India. Anything that is made in India is declared inferior products.

"Indian people are to buy only the things that are made in England. No one is allowed to buy or sell Indian things. Indian people have been losing their business. This has caused a lot of problems. So many people in India are getting poorer and poorer except a few who are wealthy and rich.

"Gandhi Ji wants to help and uplift the Indian people. So, he has started several programs that would teach people how to learn to rely on themselves and not be controlled by the greedy British people who are controlling and suppressing our people."

"We know nothing about this, Devi Ma, tell us more," said one of the girls named Chanda who was also my friend.

"One of these programs is named the Khadi revolution. Khadi means a hand spun and hand woven cloth. He tells Indian people that all of us should quit buying things that are made in England instead buy only that is made in India. Learn to spin cotton and weave your own cloth. Farmers are encouraged to plant cotton seeds and cultivate cotton and even more important do not sell your raw cotton blooms to the British merchants."

"But Devi Ma, can cotton be planted and grow in the fields?"

"Oh yes, cotton seeds are planted. The plants grow and produce the beautiful cotton buds, they bloom and produce cotton.

We can cultivate them, and the blooms are made ready to spin. And when you spin the cotton it produces threads. We use the threads to make cloth."

"Devi Ma, I see the thread coming out of cotton as you spin. I would have never known. Watching you doing this is s.................I do not know what to say."

"You do not have to say anything just watch and try to learn to spin."

"You think we can learn?"

"Of course you can learn. I would teach you. Once you learn, you can make your own yarn and weavers can change it to cloth and then you can have your own handmade garments. You would not depend on foreign cloth. You can do your own thing and be independent and in doing this you would be contributing toward the independence of your country *MOTHER INDIA!*

"Well my dear little friends that's all for today. It is time to go home for you. I will see you next Tuesday. But before you go here are some cookies I made for you." Grandma handed out the little bags that were made of her hand-spun yarn and each bag was filled with grandma's homemade cookies.

All the children gave a big hug to Grandma and said, "Yes, yes, we will come next Tuesday. Thank you so much, Devi Ma!"

And so I said to myself, "What a wonderful summer afternoon I have spent with my grandma the spinner."

Spinning churkha provides a new perspective on life. The wood that is used in creating a churkha reminds me of the significance of trees in our lives. It gives the feeling of being connected to Mother Earth who gives birth and nurtures the cotton plants who provide the spinning cotton. The process of spinning produces the thread to weave the garments we wrap around. It is fascinating to see that how every garment we wear comes out from plants "the cotton plants" that grow in soil and are nurtured with water and sunshine. The spinning of thread touches the thread of the spinner's inner core. The gentle sound of spinning almost gives the feelings of soft musical notes of string music that touches the soul.

Things That Go Bump: Triptych

By William Scott Galasso

Duff-Green mansion
Vicksburg, Mississippi
a civil war hospital
lights flicker, shadows pass
taps, whispers, taps

Charleston, S.C.
Battery Carriage House
3.A.M., floorboards creak
we wake, hearts pounding
to a long, low moan

Gettysburg, midnight
crickets chirp in the Wheat Field
the camera captures
a dozen orbs, free floating
who were you then and now

Richard Rudolf, Darling Boy

By Daphne Fineman

We, as a family, had returned from America and had begun to establish ourselves with different doctors.

In my then husband's family, there was a history of deafness and blindness, so with both pregnancies I was very careful to be alert, watching for any signs.

The first-born child was a premature baby, 4 lbs. 6oz, but thank God, he developed normally, and by one year he caught up with the other babies, except he was a poor eater.

I tried for five more years to fall pregnant and finally it happened. This wonderful baby was born, always happy, smiling at everyone, but I noticed he was not making the same baby noises that my other boy made. My cleaning lady was vacuuming in his bedroom and I mentioned to her that she might wake the baby. She replied that he never woke up when she made noise in his bedroom. So, I took two saucepans and banged them together beside him and he did not stir.

So, at eight months I made an appointment at Moorfields, which is a very famous hospital in London. They told us it was too early to make any definite diagnosis, but we should come back in six months, which we did. I already knew something was wrong but could not come to terms with it. The dreaded day came, with all the tests, and we were told that he was profoundly deaf.

We left the hospital full of disbelief, it felt like the sky had fallen onto our heads. How could this happy-go-lucky child, handsome as could be, always smiling, be deaf?

After the initial shock we had to decide what plans we should make to help him. We found a small school that would take him at five years old. By this time, we knew he was extremely smart. He was doing puzzles and adding figures in his head. Unfortunately, we found out he was dyslexic, but he was able to learn words.

One day the principal (head mistress) called me to come to the school. She first told me how smart he was, mentioning that he had all the children organized to his bidding. That he had gone into her office with a little girl called Mandy, plopped himself down into her armchair, took a needle and thread out of the teacher's drawer. Then told Mandy, "Sew my button from my shirt back on." Well the teacher said it was the funniest occurrence she had ever seen, his legs were hanging over the arm of the chair, and Mandy was following his instructions. She watched for a while and had to stop herself from laughing, while handing out a punishment to them both.

The next year she called me up to the school again. The heating had gone off in the classroom on a very cold day. Richard brought some tools from his mechanics set and set about undoing the radiator to get it working again. She was laughing, but said she had to punish him. She told me he would go far in life, because he would analyze problems and make decisions about how to go about it.

A club was formed called Kith and Kids, for children with all sorts of handicaps, physical and mental conditions such as autistic children, and those with Down's Syndrome. Richard taught them how to do up buttons and tie shoelaces, play games and generally have fun. He recognized the ones who were slow and went out of his way to help them join in.

He was fascinated with computers later on, and read schematics. He was recognized as a brain for them. When he was fifteen, he was invited to demonstrate how computers work at the British Home Show Exhibition in Kensington, London. The computer was as large as a small bedroom, and he had people surrounding his demonstration every day.

He came back to America to go to college in Freemont. To be able to go, he had to take an IQ test with a Mr. Phoenix at Pierce College, Woodland Hills. He said his IQ was at least 169 and he could be eligible for Mensa. So, of course he was accepted by the college.

He never let me know his eyesight was not good, so when they sat him in the back of the class, he could not see the blackboard clearly, but didn't complain. When he had a test the next day, he would stay up all night teaching himself and generally would pass.

Later he got a job in the IT department of a large company and worked there for ten years.

In the first few years he got along well with the staff, and he was able to get many people working in the building out of trouble when they lost all their data on their computer. He was able to save money while he was working and managed to buy a car, second hand of course, it cost him $2,000. It was his pride and joy. He did all his own repairs and kept it in tip-top conditions, and with extra mirrors he was a very good driver. He passed his driver's test without any problems.

Then calamity happened at his job. Everybody left the facility except for him, but before that happened, they put his name into an 'Achiever of the Year' program. Thousands of employees all over America were entered by their bosses. Richard was lucky enough, because of his hard work, to win. He was invited to go to Washington to meet the president. He was allowed to take a friend with him, all expenses paid. They bought him all new clothes and gave him a key to the town. Unfortunately, he never was able to meet the president because Arafat arrived there at the same time, but he did get to meet Barbara Boxer, who gave him a gift. He also met Kissinger. There were many dinners in his honor and he was made to feel very important, as everybody praised his achievements.

When he returned to California, at the building where he worked, all his friends had left, which was very disappointing. A new CEO was in charge. Some of the workers had access to the wages bills and they were resentful that Richard was earning more than they were, some of it was because he had been there much longer than them. Also, he was doing a more complicated job than they were.

Richard started to notice that some of the computer programs were missing, but he did nothing about it, until the CEO sent all the staff a letter stating that if any employee saw people taking anything out of the facility, they <u>must</u> report it. Richard, not being worldly, and a little naïve, reported that some computer programs had been taken out and not returned to the office. Well, that was the beginning of the end for Richard, life was all downhill after that for him. The

CEO called him into his office and asked him who took the programs, and he told him Phillip Runnels. The boss thanked him for being honest and said he would deal with it, and the programs would be returned for Richard's use. My husband and I were invited to the facility for a progress report on our son. When we were leaving Phillip stopped us in the hallway and said, "Your son nearly ruined my career and I will do the same to him." I replied, "The CEO asked all the employees if they saw anybody removing the programs or data form the building, they must let him know, and Richard, not being very sophisticated, believed it was his duty to tell."

Several years later I went to the DMV with Richard to renew his license for driving, and he told me he only wanted to renew his ID since his eyesight was not good enough to see clearly for driving, and that he did not want to hurt anyone. I know what a heart-wrenching situation this was for him, as he loved his car so much. He confided to me he would love to get married and have children. His nature is so sweet and kind and also so honest, never having told me a lie in all his life. I pray to the Lord this will happen someday; he would make a wonderful father.

Around this time, Phillip was made manager. He would go away for several days, and lock several room doors. Richard would have to wait until he returned to get in there in order to repair employees' computers. Phillip started saying it was dangerous for Richard to be in there, but it was not, he was familiar with every inch of the rooms. The next nasty thing Phillip did was to take Richard's office, which had a window and was quite large and airy. Phillip opened a broom closet with a table and chair and stuck Richard in there. One day, the CEO told Phillip that the staff could go home early after lunch, as the next day was a holiday. But he did not let Richard know. That day Richard thought that he hadn't felt any vibrations for a couple of hours and went around looking to see if he could find anyone, but everybody had left. A cleaning lady told Richard the bus left at lunchtime and she also called me to pick him up.

The following week I called the office and asked Phillip why he didn't let Richard know. He started to laugh and thought it was very funny. I told him he was a very mean man to do that to a deaf person who did not see well. He just shrugged and said Richard should leave the job. But Richard loved his job and put up with all of Phillip's insults. After that Phillip moved the air conditioner unit over the roof of Richard's office, so the whole closet vibrated. He was hoping Richard would leave. When he didn't, he made a plan for everything to be outsourced at another facility so he could close the computer office down. He told Richard he would have to leave, as the work for computers would be outsourced. So, he made good on his promise to us that one day he would get rid of Richard.

Of course, it was very difficult for him to find another job, deaf and legally blind. He wrote beautiful resumes with his ability to type at 140 words per minute. He converted the computer to very large script, but eventually he lost much more eyesight, and went completely blind.

He memorized all the freeways and streets within a fifty-mile radius and let me know which route to take by printing it out on the computer. The government let him use his 401K to purchase a home, affordable housing, of course. He lavished care on his home keeping it spotlessly clean, using the vacuum and polishing the furniture, keeping all the drawers tidy, and cleaning the toilets. Later on, he put some simple plants on his patio, but he had difficulty in keeping the timer on the clock working regularly. So, he redid the electricals and removed everything to his computer and never had another problem. His kitchen sink had bad leaks, he asked me to take him to Home Depot to buy the parts he needed. He felt every pipe he needed and I wondered how it could be possible that he could know what he was doing. But sure enough, I watched him take out every pipe, lay them out in sequence, put in the new pipes, and miraculously the faucet never again leaked.

He decided he needed a cover for his computer made of leather. Of course, we could not find one. But at Michael's store a young man helped us find a leather store in Costa Mesa. Richard felt all the leather, of course, and found one that was just hard enough. He bought it then asked for a leather needle and leather sewing tape. I was astounded, I did not know such a thing existed. The store owner was also astounded and asked him to show it to him when it was completed. Within one week he showed it to me too. I asked him how he measured it and he told me he used the width of his hand.

He never ceases to amaze me. He went to school for one year to learn Braille, and learned very quickly.

The Syrophoenician Woman
"Royalty and Loyalty, Women Who Loved the Lord"
By Daneen Pysz

The Introduction

"Let the children be fed first. For it is not right to take the food of the children and throw it to the dogs." This statement has bothered many people at first reading, because it sounds as if Jesus is being rude and flippant to the Syrophoenician Woman. I don't believe that was the case. In my book, *"Royalty and Loyalty,"* this unnamed woman showed a great deal of loyalty. Not only in her mission to search out Jesus to heal her daughter, but also in her willingness to humble herself before our Lord and Savior when she believed his words would heal.

The story of the Syrophoenician woman is found in the Gospel of Matthew 15:21-28 and the Gospel of Mark 6:24-30. Both Gospels place her story right in the middle of their Books. Matthew focused his writings towards the Jewish people, and Mark wrote for the Gentiles. Mark placed this story as a bridge for the cultural differences of Jews and Greeks/Gentiles to be the focal point of Jesus' ministry and saving grace for all people.

The story is multilayered with additional lessons for the disciples and possibly for Jesus. Here is a confrontation/imploring of the Gentile woman for healing of her demon-possessed daughter. It speaks volumes about her faith. On another level, the disciples oftentimes, did not exhibit that volume of faith. Many times, they misunderstood Jesus' message asking for clarification on many parables. Finally, perhaps Jesus, being fully human, was drained from his recent encounter with the Pharisees and simply needed Divine inspiration compelled by the Gentile woman to remind him that his message was meant for everyone.

Women, children, orphans, the afflicted, the poor and widows were used throughout the New Testament to bring attention to what Jesus wanted people to know. Jesus' mission was for all people. The Syrophoenician woman shows courage and bravery in her conversation with Jesus and her qualities are recognized by Jesus as faith.

We don't know this woman's name, if she was married or a widow, wealthy, poor, or if she had other children. St. Mark only tells us of the region she was from and she was searching for Jesus; probably because she had heard of his preaching and miracles. In Mark 3:8, we read, "When they heard about all he was doing, many people came to him from Judea, Jerusalem, Idumea, and the regions across the Jordan and around Tyre and Sidon."

Because Jesus traveled into Gentile territory, it gave the Syrophoenician Woman the opportunity to go and seek him out. Her desperate situation opened her heart to reach out to Jesus and let him into her life. She didn't know it at the time, but her actions showed she was ready and willing to accept him. His love and salvation has no prejudices or borders. He is the same with a man or a woman, rich or poor, servant or master, Jew or Gentile. We should learn this lesson for how we treat others. Jesus has crossed over into each of our lives. Are you ready and willing to meet and accept him?

Using the story found in Mark 7:24-30, outside sources, and inspiration from the Holy Spirit; here is the final *"Royalty and Loyalty"* story. Her loyalty was her love and fortitude to get her child well by searching for Jesus.

The Syrophoenician Woman: The Story

Peace to you sisters and brothers—

I am another unnamed woman in the Bible, but I came to be known as the "Syrophoenician Woman." This name encompassed both the territories of Syria and ancient Phoenicia, which now represented the northern Greek Hellenistic culture. To some, I might have been known as the 'psychophoenician woman' because of my crazy, out of character actions of approaching a Jewish man, who also happened to be a Rabbi; which was unheard of by a Gentile woman.

You see, the culture of the Jews and the Greeks had many parallel similarities when it came to how men and women lived.

However, when it came to religion, the Jews considered the Greeks unclean because of the types of food they ate and pagans because they worshipped idols. My story meshes together the social classes of Jews and Gentiles, men and women, servanthood and authority, and shame and honor. Women were in marginal roles and subservient to men in both cultures.

Throughout history, the Jews have been segregated by religion and class distinction. Although many Greeks/Gentiles worshipped in the outer Temple of the Jews, the Jews still did not consider them to be God's chosen people. Religious purity and cleanliness rules were two deciding factors that separated the Greeks from the Jews.

There was a long history of discourse and animosity against the people of Tyre, which was where I encountered Jesus and the Jewish culture. The prophet Isaiah spoke about the people of Tyre saying they had no allotment in the Messianic banquet and must be destroyed for the vindication of Israel. The Jews associated both and Sidon, which was further north, as communities resembling ancient Sodom and Gomorrah.

The Gentile people in Tyre were considered the enemy of the Jews. Tyre was economically powerful and wealthy, and was the oppressor to the rural Jewish communities of God's chosen people. In his Gospel, the Apostle Mark clearly identifies me as being from this ancient, wealthy Hellenistic culture and my Syrophoenician religious practices. My race were descendants of Ham, Noah's son, and were first known as the Canaanites.

Talk about setting the stage for a courageous story! Some might have thought me to be a wee bit psycho, but that didn't bother me. All I knew was my daughter, Iris, was sick and had a demon in her; and I wanted my baby girl well again. The Apostle Mark called this demon an unclean spirit, probably to emphasize the fact the Greeks were unclean to the Jews. Jesus' fame of his ministry and healings had spread throughout Tyre and Sidon. I overheard some Jews saying Jesus was leaving Capernaum and heading to Tyre, which was north about thirty-five miles. I set my plan in motion to seek him out.

I'm not exactly sure how I found Jesus, but I believe something kept guiding me in a specific direction until I found and saw him enter into a house. I had no idea who owned the house or who else would be there. I just saw the back of Jesus entering. Now you might be asking, "How did she know that was Jesus? Did she see him preach before?" Great questions; I would be skeptical and ask those questions, too! I can't explain it, except it was a feeling, an intuition that compelled me to follow my instincts and just move forward. I was a woman on a mission to seek out the only person I believed who could and would heal my daughter.

Jesus' disciples were outside talking about a discussion he and the Pharisees had on the rituals of cleanliness related to purity prior to coming to Tyre. The Pharisees thought of cleanliness on the outside with the ritual of hand washing, and Jesus taught cleanliness was found within a person. The disciples seemed to be a bit confused as to what point Jesus was trying to make. I was not sure what to make of this dialogue as all that resonated within me were the words "clean and unclean." Here I was, a Gentile; considered unclean by Jews, and going into a strange house to speak with this Jewish Rabbi.

My heart was pounding in my throat, and I felt as if I would explode. Would this man speak to me? As I said before, Jewish men did not speak directly to women; especially Greek women. Even though my Syrophoenician background gave me some entitlements of honor within my community, I knew they would not serve any redeeming purpose for my encounter with Jesus.

I entered and saw him reclining at the table with his head bowed; I think he was praying. I waited for a few moments trying to keep my courage up and not wanting to interrupt; all the while aware of the small window of time I had before the disciples would enter. I let out a deep breath and rushed over to him and fell at his feet begging, "Have mercy on me, O Lord, Son of David! I beg you to drive the demon out of my daughter."

Both the Jewish and Greek cultures possess the qualities of honor and shame along with authority and servanthood. By falling to Jesus' feet, I showed a position of shame and servanthood giving him the position of honor and authority. In doing this, I acknowledged he was the Messiah for the Jews.

Just then his disciples entered and a couple of them rudely said, "Tell her to go away. She is bothering us with all her begging." However, Jesus did not send me away as he didn't seem bothered at all by my begging.

He didn't answer me immediately. The silence was deafening. I knew I was putting Jesus in an uncomfortable position to acknowledge me. Culturally, it would make him look foolish for speaking to a woman by answering my plea. It was as if I startled him out of his solitude. But then he acknowledged my subservient position and we became equals in our conversation.

Jesus' response was not of a typical Rabbi, for he said, "Let the children be fed first. For it is not right to take the food of the children and throw it to the dogs."

At first, his words were a bit harsh and confusing to me. I immediately thought; what does he mean by "food, children, dogs?" Everything I had ever heard about him was how kind and good he was to everyone. I had never heard anyone say Jesus called people dogs.

The Jews did consider dogs to be unclean and scavengers, and from my Greek friends who followed Jesus, I knew he was referring to the Jews as the children and food was his message of salvation. Some of my Greek friends took part in the miracle feeding of the five thousand, and they shared that message and many other miracle stories with me.

The word dog was still a bit harsh to most ears, but to Greeks-- dogs, especially little dogs, were pets and endearing to us. All this information flashed through my mind in a couple of seconds. All I could humbly reply was, "Lord, even the dogs under the table eat the children's scraps."

We Gentiles were like the sweet little dogs who were happy and faithful for the scraps from the Jewish Messiah. My answer seemed to satisfy Jesus, and he commended me and said, "For saying this, you may go. The demon has gone out of your daughter."

That short conversation with Jesus ignited my faith. He saw my clean and pure heart and recognized my faith in him. He didn't even need to see my daughter, just his words healed her.

When I arrived home, my precious baby girl greeted me with laughter and smiles. My neighbor friend, Julia cried out, "Your sweet Iris is healed. Did you go to find Jesus like I told you to do?" "Yes," I said. "He was so kind and respectful to me—a Gentile woman. When did Iris start feeling better?"

"About noon today," Julia said.

"That was about the time I was speaking with Jesus!" I exclaimed. "What a miracle!"

I was on cloud nine for the next week and wanted to see Jesus again. Iris said, "Momma, tell me more about Jesus. Do you think his message is for us too? Can you take me to see him?" "Yes," I said, "I believe it is for us, too. He told me my faith was great for what I had said and done." So, I told her I would see if he was still in Tyre.

My friends told me he had healed a deaf man in up in Sidon, and he was heading back to the Sea of Galilee. I had to see him again, so Iris and I went with my friends to find him. We caught up with a large crowd on the outskirts of Gentile territory. Just like the previous miracle of Jesus feeding five thousand people, Jesus again performed the miracle of feeding many people. My friend Gaius took a quick survey of the people and said, "I lost count after four thousand men. I didn't even get to count all of the women and children, there are so many. Jesus is ministering to the Gentiles! Salvation is for us, too!"

My life was changed when I met Jesus and realized he had entered my heart. Many of the Jewish people didn't understand his teachings, and they wanted to make him their earthly king. Jesus' traveling from Jewish territory was the best thing for the Gentiles. I believe God placed me before his Son, to rekindle Jesus' Spirit that his message of Salvation was for everyone.

It wasn't long after Jesus left Gentile territory and returned to Jerusalem that I heard his own people crucified him. At first, I didn't understand why he had to die such a horrible death.

Eventually, other disciples and even the Apostle Paul, came to Sidon and shared the good and glorious news of Jesus' resurrection.

That first encounter with Jesus proved to be significant as Mark used my story of the Syrophoencian race to build the connecting line for all cultures. This showed Christ's love, acceptance, and salvation for all people.

Because Jesus traveled into Gentile territory where I lived, it gave me the opportunity to go and seek him out. My desperate situation opened my heart to reach out to Jesus and let him into my life. I didn't know it at the time, but my actions showed I was ready and willing to accept him. His love and salvation has no prejudices or borders. He is the same with a man or a woman, rich or poor, servant or master. We should learn this lesson for how we treat others.

Zeke the Rooster
By Margaret Estrada

This is a story told by my father, Ralph Arthur Allen, about his Grandfather, Andrew Jackson O'Neal. Back in the early 1900's, my father, Ralph, at age 4, lived with his parents, Arthur Lewis Allen and Bertie O'Neal Allen, and his sister, Margaret, on a farm near Madison, Kansas. During the years leading to the great depression, and by the year 1910, farming was becoming difficult financially, so Arthur began looking for new opportunities for his family out west.

Arthur had several brothers who were living in Glendale, California, a rural town near Los Angeles, and who owned a home and operated a feed store business. Arthur's plan was to travel with his family, and hopefully purchase a small parcel of land in California. Arrangements were made, and the family and all of their belongings traveled from Kansas by train to Glendale, where they stayed for a time with relatives. They eventually bought a piece of property, which looked very lovely in the black and white photo. The property was in Delano, over 100 miles north of Glendale in California's Central Valley on dry desert land.

Then, with their family and household belongings loaded on an open wagon, they traveled north over mountain roads, down into the Central Valley, to the plot of land out in the desert just outside of Delano. On the property there was a small house, but not much else. My grandfather, Arthur, who was creative in using what was available, added an upstairs room to the little house, and built a few out-buildings, including a chicken coop and yard. He and his wife, Bertie O'Neal Allen, raised their two children, Margaret and Ralph on the little ranch. They had chickens, a few cows, and rabbits, and my grandfather worked on other farms in the area to keep food on the table.

When my dad was in his teens, his grandfather, Andrew Jackson O'Neal, known as "Pa Jack", came from Kansas to live with the family for a while. Being widowed, he was spending his retirement years living with each of his grown children, as was the custom in their family. Grandpa Jack used to enjoy sitting outside in the summer where the intense heat was modified by a nearby tree and an occasional breeze. In those days, there were farms and pastures all around in the valley, and flies were everywhere. Grandpa Jack used to sit outside in his chair near the chicken yard and watch the chickens, while he swatted the pesky flies that swarmed around him. It was cooler outside the small house than inside, where screens kept the flies out. Besides, being an old farmer, he enjoyed watching the chickens and their antics.

One day, while sitting under the tree swatting the flies, Pa Jack noticed that the roosters and other chickens were attacking one young rooster, who was barely old enough to have very many feathers. The chickens would gang up on this little rooster and peck at him until he was a mass of sores and feathers sticking out in all directions. Pa Jack felt very sad for the little rooster who was being treated so badly. One day, the chickens cornered the little rooster against the chicken wire fence, where he was attacked repeatedly, until suddenly, the little rooster was pushed so hard that he found himself out from under the chicken wire fence, and into the yard where he was free!

The poor little rooster wasn't sure of where he was or what to do. He was hungry, thirsty, and confused, not to mention frightened! Pa Jack was watching all of this drama from his "front row seat" under the tree, and felt great empathy for the little rooster. After some time, Pa Jack tried tossing a fly over to where the little rooster was cowering. The rooster watched, noticed the fly, and finally, cautiously, eased himself over to it, and grabbed the fly. Pa Jack was fascinated, and tossed him another fly, which was quickly eaten by the rooster.

Eventually, Pa Jack gave the rooster the name "Zeke". He continued to talk gently to Zeke and feed him flies. Zeke finally got the idea that this old man was not his enemy, but his friend and Zeke began to move closer and closer to where Pa Jack was sitting. As the hot summer days passed, Zeke was living freely outside of the chicken coop in the yard, where he and Pa Jack developed quite a friendship. Zeke's sore places began to heal, and his feathers became sleek and healthy like any full grown rooster's feathers should.

As the months passed, Zeke learned it was safe to sit on Pa Jack's lap out in the yard, where he would continue to eat the flies that he swatted. In fact the two became such good friends that Zeke would sit on Pa Jack's shoulder when he walked around the yard. When Zeke had fully grown his feathers as an adult rooster, he was reintroduced to the chicken yard. After adjusting to this change, Zeke was finally accepted by the other chickens, and was able to "hold his own" as a grown rooster. He no longer was intimidated by the other roosters, and according to my dad, Zeke became the "head rooster".

To me, this story could be a metaphor for our own lives. As children and adolescents, we grew and learned to stand up for ourselves with the help of a parent, or a mentor, and because of their caring we have become the persons we are today through our life experiences.

My Goals and Aspirations
By Dorothy G. Kuhr

At eighty years of life, my goals and aspirations seem to have no value. I do not have the time to see them through--or do I?

Is it too late?

Experience taught me perseverance, hope and know-how.
Did it teach me what I needed to learn: to love and be loved?

When I was a child I wanted most to be cherished and loved.
Yet I never felt worthy to be loved.

Those who loved me dearly could never love me enough, for I did not have the self-love to be loved. If I find it,

is it too late to make a difference?

Role models were far and too few, leaving me hopeless and disappointed.

I have always been capable of accomplishing whatever I deemed important. Achieving purpose, meaning , creativity and love did not fulfill my ideal self-aspirations.

My greatest accomplishment is to be the cherished and loved mother that I am and had desperately wanted to be.

What goals and aspirations? What legacy would I like to create? I just want to love and be loved.

I don't believe it is too late.

A Dream Come True

By Sunshine Lutey

It was November 6, 2018; Sunshine had just finished the video of the Sunshine Performance Club's October 2018 Show. As she and David watched the video on their big screen television, David interrupted, "Hold it, Sunshine; I have an idea."

Sunshine paused the video and David continued, "Why don't we do a show with just you and me in June – a 'Sunshine and Raindrop' show."

Sunshine responded adamantly, "No, honey; we already have a charity show scheduled for October 6, 2019. I can't do two shows in one year."

Later she pondered, "He's a wonderful singer; because we had so many good entertainers in the last show he only performed one solo. He's going to be 95 in a few months. Why am I saying 'No' to this wonderful man?"

In the morning, she scheduled a June 9, 2019 show and began to plan a program to fulfill his dream.

Two weeks later on November 19, David entered the house from the garage and sat down in his favorite living room chair. "David," Sunshine grumbled crossly, "last night you promised you would practice our songs today and you've been doing everything but that!"

She looked at him. His face was pale; he was rubbing his right arm. With concern she asked gently, "David, what's wrong?" He tried to respond but his words were garbled. She dialed 911 and the firetruck arrived within minutes. The medical team at the hospital cared for him well and he survived with very little damage from the stroke. He suffered mini-strokes in March and recovered well. However, they discovered there was damage when they began to rehearse for the show; he couldn't remember all the lyrics – knowing his lyrics had been one of his talents.

Sunshine questioned, "Shall I cancel the show?"

David vehemently replied, "Don't say things like that!"

They began to rehearse two hours daily; little by little his ability to retain lyrics grew.

Sunshine called the show a "Once in a Lifetime Event" -- a unique, never before attempted charity show that David wanted to share with the Village as well as with family and friends. They invited an excellent pianist, Jackie O'Neill to join them and together they created the 90-minute show -- "An Evening of Song" which

was preceded by a one-hour historical video that Sunshine created.

The video started with the inception of the Village in 1964.

It then traced the musical trail since David, (1994) and Sunshine (1995) came to the Village, through 2019.

Sunshine also created scenes that displayed at the back of the stage for every song and with the help of four club members and family, the show proceeded smooth as silk.

Yes, on June 9, 2019 a dream came true for David "Raindrop" Hartman and Sunshine Lutey.

What's That You Were Saying?

By Dennis Glauber

In the 32 plus years that we lived in Seattle, one of the most (if not *the* most) involving cultural experience was with the Seattle Chamber Music Society. I had attended every single concert since its inception in 1982 and my wife Evette served for many years on the Board of Directors in many capacities including the presidency. For the first twenty years or so the annual Summer Festival was held at the prestigious Lakeside School in north Seattle, alma mater of such luminaries as the famous founders of Microsoft and Cellular One. My story today concerns a singular event when building alterations at Lakeside forced that year's festival to relocate to the nearby Shorecrest School. The event to which I refer was much talked about and was mentioned in the concert reviews in both of Seattle's daily newspapers.

Several years later, for the compilation of a celebratory book on the history of the Society and its founder, I recalled the incident in the following lines of verse

Of my many memories, one of the best
Concerns a certain night at Shorecrest
When there we all sat with our programs before us
Astonished to hear an unscheduled chorus

That year our tenure at Lakeside had ceased
Their builders had forced us a mile to the east
The show must go on....is the Golden Rule
So, we settled in at Shorecrest School

Our musicians played with their usual feeling
Until they were joined up there in the ceiling
By voices that kept getting higher and higher.
The festival now had a heavenly choir!

Some of us cried "hush", others just said "shoo"
And others just shrugged, what else can you do?
When asked how long they meant to be part of the score
By way of reply they just quoth "Evermore"

One thing I will say for our feathered friends
They sure know how to pursue their own ends
So, let's add to each program the following words,
"Sometimes chamber music really is for the birds!"

Now the irony of my little poem is that apparently alone among the hundreds there, I actually did not hear a single tweet, chirp or note of birdsong, and I was dissembling madly when joining in all the discussion of the birds in the rooftop. For all this was long before the day when I finally grappled with my failing ability to hear, and started the process that led to my acquisition of hearing aids. Like so many others before me, I had resisted, went into a state of denial and found reasons to blame others for not speaking clearly. It was always the inferior cordless phone at fault, never me. My situation was not quite equal to that of my late brother-in-law. He finally acceded to his family's demands that he see his physician. When told by the good doctor to return the following day for a hearing test he arrived with a full specimen bottle. The doctor said "I don't have to test you, my friend. You NEED hearing aids. I told you to come for a hearing test, not a urine test!"

There is something macho about denying the fading of one's hearing that never seems to apply to problems of vision and the correction thereof. Almost everybody wears glasses for some, or all daily activities, but somehow many of us feel that hearing aids are an acknowledgment that from here on its downhill all the way. I was even encouraged in denial by my physician who made no bones about his own resolve to avoid auditory "crutches" for as long as possible lest he become increasingly dependent on them.

Over the last sixteen years with a succession of increasingly sophisticated hearing aids, a generous supply of batteries and minus several thousand dollars, I have been able to enjoy conversations at a whole new level. I have found film soundtracks to be vastly improved and have gained so much in the pursuit of my favorite cultural hobby, namely listening to music in the concert hall and the opera house. With the newest state of the art hearing aids the use of cellphones does not present a problem. The only negatives are the increased noise levels in crowded situations, even with the program designed to reduce that problem.

I have resisted all blandishments to get smaller, almost invisible aids

I need aids, here they are

I need reading glasses, here they are

I need my cane, here it is

(My answer when asked 'What's with the cane?' is "I'm no longer Abel.")

That is the limited me, the partially disabled me, and I am content.

So it's time for a toast to my various audiologists over the years, a toast to which I can only echo

HEAR, HEAR!

My UniVerse

By B.D. Faw

I love songbirds and tall trees and soft summer winds
    blowing warmly across my face;
I love happy young puppies and mellow old cats
    and hummingbirds frozen in grace;

I like walking alone, with interior eyes
    viewing scenery the world can't conceive;
And extended discussions with Ego and Id
    while exploring what we might believe;

I don't care much for money--but still must admit
    that a few things gold buys can be nice;
And, while treasuring solitude, often it's clear
    that my internal peace has its price.

My cosmos embraces the sighs of the sad,
    and the tears of the mortally grieving;
The joys of salvation; the final despair
    when one can't continue believing.

Yet my life is my own (for I've made it that way);
    It's all that I've dreamed it could be.
I go where I wish and I do as I please
    and I know what it's like to be free.

But my world's at its best when I share with a guest
    in my heart what eternity wove.
For, alone's not enough--when I'm through playing tough--
    I simply love being In Love!

Life in a File

By Peggy P Edwards

She had the uncanny ability to organize people's lives and put them in files. She tried to do the same with her own family's lives. But they filled so many files, the files soon started taking over her own life.

Each file held a year starting with the 1790 Census – aka, the first year of the great File. Circa 1775 her great, great, and three more greats, grandfather, Jacques de Russy arrived in America from France, to fight with Lafayette in the American Revolution. He fell in love with the wildness, the infinite possibilities and a woman named Sarah.

In 1790 he and his wife, Sarah, appeared in the first American Census with his new anglophile name, James Russey. They begat for several generations, and someone in the family was always sure to keep records.

They settled in Winchester Tennessee; the next generations moved throughout the country: Texas, Florida, the Carolinas, Wisconsin, Kentucky, Georgia, and finally California. They even extended their patrimony to Mexico.

They were soldiers, masons, miners, firemen, actors, doctors, dentists, builders, plantation owners, train conductors, pastors, attorneys and teachers. They fought in the Revolution, the Civil War, World War I and II and the Middle East. They were officers in the Army, Navy and Air Force.

Her great uncle, Alfred Crowel, organized and was captain of America's first soccer team in Mexico. Her maternal grandfather transformed the mule-driven silver mines of Pachuca, Mexico to electricity (which he learned from Thomas A. Edison). Her great uncle founded the first General Motors franchise in Mexico City. Her paternal grandfather was killed by Pancho Villa at the border.

She was saddened by the fact that the women were hardly mentioned beyond their married name, although one was a well-known stage actress in New York. The truth was her grandmother was the family's great adventurer and through her travels and insights, helped make the rest of the family rich after she settled in Hollywood.

Because she became accepted by the family as their historian, they sent her family treasures to fit into her files. She heard the voices of those who came before her. She saw it as her obligation to make those voices heard, and so they traveled through the centuries so they too could be remembered and recognized in the present.

Eventually she realized she was living in retrospect, but she was obsessed with the past, which she knew existed. She couldn't say the same about the future.

Occasions When I Possibly Could Have Died

By Larry Johnston

1. *When a train almost ran me over.* I was around eleven years old. A friend and I were walking along the base of a sixty-foot-tall rocky bluff along the Mississippi River in South St. Louis, Missouri. We had climbed the sheer, seventy-foot bluff to look out over the river from what we thought was a Civil War gun emplacement. There were three sets of tracks along the bluff going around a curve. We were walking between the tracks of the set closest to the bluff wall.

A loud train whistle began sounding short blasts from around the curve behind us. We instinctively began running to a long set of steps that led back up to the street to the top of the bluff. The horn became louder. It was now constantly blowing. We ran faster and didn't think to look behind us. The horn's sound then became deafening. I yelled to my friend to jump to the wall, four feet away, and grab a small tree [sprout] trunk growing out from the wall. We both made the jump and within seconds the train flew by, the wind almost pulling at our small scared bodies. We were both now hanging from a sprout rooted into the rock wall. The loud rumbling train was speeding past our back sides for what seemed like forever.

I think we both had pissed in our pants. After the train passed, we turned loose of the small trees we both had grabbed onto. We had been walking between the rails of the tracks the train had been traveling on. We somewhat regained our senses and on wobbly legs, walked to the long stairway leading up the sixty to seventy feet to South Broadway Street. We climbed the stairs, returned home while still somewhat startled. We never told our parents about that experience.

2. *When I fell off a horse.* I was around twelve years old and riding a horse while at my uncle's farm. My cousin, Bobby Joe, and I were riding bare-back and racing the horses back to the house. Both horses quickly turned left at the driveway to the house. I slid off my horse and landed on the ground. The horse stopped, above me, with

its front hooves flailing wildly above my body, face and head. I was laying on my back. I began waving my arms and kicking my legs at the horse's stomach while trying to avoid its hooves. The horse then leapt over my body and I was spared a crushed body or head injury. Bobby had remained on his horse. Neither of us told our parents about the incident.

3. *When a horse fell over backward.* I was around thirteen years old working on a horse ranch owned by a doctor. While riding a young gelding horse on a small incline, I pulled the reins back to make him stop. The horse then suddenly reared up and fell over backwards. I pushed myself away from the saddle when the horse was standing upright, on its two hind legs. It lost its balance and was falling over backward and I was falling too. I had pushed my body away before the horse fell and we both hit the ground. I was on my ass about two feet away from the horse's head, when it hit the ground. We both then got upright and were not injured. Had I not pushed my body away, the horse would have landed on me and probably crushed me to death.

4. *When I was driving a tractor and it slid off the road.* I was around fourteen years old and driving a Ford tractor near full speed on a gravel road. It was raining hard and I was racing to a fence line to close a gate.

While going downhill on a road, along a ridge, I hit just the right wheel brake pedal; not the right and left brake pedals simultaneously. The right rear wheel locked causing the tractor to slide to the right and off the road. It came to a stop on the downhill sloped edge of the road. It was now leaning precariously over to its right. I slowly stepped off to the left and jumped to the flat road area. I was completely soaked and shaking. I had almost turned the tractor over. It could have gone over and down on top of me while it rolled over sideways down the hill. I walked, in the pouring rain, back to the barn for help, and another tractor to pull the Ford back up on the road.

5. *When a motor scooter flipped over and threw me in a ditch*. I was around fifteen years old. A friend, Artie, and I were riding on his Cushman Scooter. He was driving it way too fast around a curve on a gravel road. He lost control. We both were thrown airborne and landed in a roadside ditch. The scooter came to rest in the middle of the road. It was upside down resting on the seat and handlebars, and still running while in that position. We turned it up-right and rode it back to his house. We had escaped being injured.

6. *When I consumed gin through a straw*. I was around seventeen years old. My friend and I were planning to go dancing and wanted to get to feeling good early. We both obtained a ½ pint bottle of gin and decided to drink it straight, through a straw, absent any mixer. We accomplished the task, went dancing and continued consuming alcohol for the rest of the night. We bunked at his house and in the morning his mother woke us up. She stated the room smelled so strong of alcohol, she thought we had both died from alcohol poisoning. I never consumed Gin after that time, but I did get somewhat drunk on a few occasions.

7. *When my submarine possibly hit an underwater mine*. I was around nineteen years old. I was aboard the submarine U.S.S. Queenfish, SS 393, somewhere in the south China Sea. We were submerged moving along at maybe four knots when we heard a loud bang on the port [left] side outer hull. The sound was like a sledgehammer hitting the steel outer buoyancy tanks. Everyone aboard heard the noise.

A few seconds later it happened again for five to six times all along the outer port hull, from the bow [front] to the stern [back], as we moved through the water. The duty officer sounded the emergency alarms and ordered the boat to surface. The Queenfish surfaced and stopped out in the middle of nowhere. There was nothing in sight in any direction. Lookouts scanned the water and saw no vessels anywhere. The boat continued on the surface to Korea. Most guys aboard thought we had hit a WW II mine that was still suspended underwater. [Now sixteen years after the war had ended.] The object had bounced off the sub's hull numerous times. If it had been an old underwater mine, lucky for us, it did not explode.

8. *When I fell asleep driving Route 66 in Oklahoma.* I was around twenty-one years old. I had purchased a 1959 Pontiac Bonneville and was driving to Missouri from San Diego. After being up all day working on the submarine, I went on leave for three weeks. I left San Diego heading east at three PM on a Friday. After driving alone, all night, I picked up two hitch-hiking sailors early Saturday, somewhere in the middle of Arizona. The plan was for them to keep me awake as I didn't want either of them to drive, for insurance reasons.

I drove all day Saturday along Route 66 through Arizona, New Mexico and into Texas. I stopped briefly for fuel, drinks and restroom breaks. I felt myself dozing off frequently on Saturday but I managed to stay alert and continue eastbound. The two sailors had settled in the back seat and slept for the entire trip. They woke up for the short times when I made stops and then they both quickly fell asleep again. My smoking cigarettes, drinking coffee, popping No-Doze pills and drinking soda kept me awake. I did blink my eyes, put a wet rag on my face and slap my face frequently to keep alert.

Somewhere in Oklahoma, I really fell asleep while driving around seventy miles per hour. I was startled awake by a car traveling behind me. The driver was sounding their car's horn constantly to get my attention and that woke me up. I think the driver had been watching me maybe swerving on the road for some time. I was still on the straight roadway. I waved at the driver and pulled over to walk around the car a bit. I then drove on to Joplin, Missouri. It was now around midnight on Saturday. I told the two sailors good-bye. I rented a motel room where I slept for twelve hours. I had spent about thirty-three hours driving from California.

9. *When my submarine was sinking backwards.* I was around twenty-three years old. Now stationed aboard the submarine, U.S.S. Menhaden, SS 377, somewhere in the ocean north of Japan. We had

101

been submerged for four to five weeks. The boat had hit a place in the water where the salt content and temperature had changed drastically. Now being negative buoyancy, [too heavy] we began to sink backwards. I was in the after-torpedo room [back of the boat] when the alarms sounded. I jumped out of my bunk and shut the water-tight door into the maneuvering room. The electricians there had pulled the speed sticks to all-ahead flank, or full speed ahead!

We were still sinking backward as I was watching a depth gauge on the bulkhead [wall]. The stern [after torpedo room] was now five hundred feet underwater. The boat's test depth was four hundred twelve feet. I knew we were sinking. I remember a fleeting thought; how I could send my mother a letter to tell her what had happened to me. The officer in the control room was having tanks blown to get us back to a positive buoyancy. Also setting the two propellers speed at all ahead flank.

Within a short while we stopped sinking and started moving up closer to the surface. The boat finally gained speed and levelled off above its test depth. We continued on our trip and later arrived in Japan. [The navy lost the submarine U. S. S. Sculpin in the north Atlantic earlier in 1963, with one hundred and twenty-nine men aboard.]

10. *When I was standing among high-voltage, street-light wires.* I was around twenty-nine years old. I was working as a Jackson, Missouri policeman at a major accident scene. It was close to six PM. A tractor trailer had jack-knifed on a very stormy and rainy night along a highway through town. The larger truck crossed the highway and hit a Chevy panel type truck head-on. The larger truck's driver was out of the cab and standing along the side of the road. He was not injured. A forty-foot, high-wire light pole had been broken and it laid across the highway. Wires were all around the area and across the small panel truck's body.

I arrived and contacted the driver of the panel truck, still seated behind the wheel. His front seat passenger was in the back of the unit and I determined he was most likely dead. I was talking to the driver who was barely coherent and in shock. I had my hands on the bottom of his door frame window area, as the window had been broken out. I was talking with him and waiting for an ambulance to arrive. A city worked yelled telling me, "Take your hands off the truck! There will be sixty-thousand volts coming through the wires any minute now, the lights are scheduled to come on at six PM. The guy will be all right. The rubber truck tires will protect him from being grounded. You will be electrocuted by holding on to the metal vehicle and standing on the wet highway!" I quickly removed my hands from the vehicle.

A few minutes passed, and the city worker then told me the wires had been cut and were safe now. The man could be removed from the truck. The ambulance team quickly removed the man from the driver's seat area and took him to the hospital. The coroner arrived and removed the deceased person's body. I called for tow trucks, made a detailed accident report and had the highway cleared of all debris.

11. *When my VW bus was almost hit from behind.* I was around twenty-eight years old and driving along Highway 55 toward St. Louis Missouri at about eleven PM. In the VW van's passenger seat was my wife. Sleeping in the back, above the engine compartment, was our four-year-old son. We were heading to my in-law's house.

I was driving about sixty-five miles per hour in the center lane of three northbound lanes. The traffic was light, as it was late. In my rear-view mirror, I saw two headlights approaching very fast from behind my van. The driver was possibly going ninety to one hundred miles per hour. I told my wife to hold on. I hit the brakes and pulled over to the right, still going too fast to stop or drive off the paved surface.

Within seconds, the approaching vehicle slid sideways around the left side of my VW van. It continued past me, still sliding almost sideways, at a high rate of speed. A passenger in the sedan was yelling out the open window as the car passed. Within a couple seconds the car fish-tailed, swerved some and then continued straight on along the highway. I pulled the van back into the slow lane. I was somewhat pissed and shaken over the incident. We were all okay.

12. *When my VW van was hit by a glass bottle.* I was around thirty years old and driving my VW van south on a two-lane highway in Missouri. It was mid-afternoon and my wife and son were in the vehicle with me. I was driving about sixty miles per hour. Traffic in both directions was light. Suddenly I heard a very loud bang, like a shotgun or tire blowing out. The VW still drove fine. I didn't feel any problems with the steering. I quickly pulled over and walked all around the van.

On the van's front driver's side, I saw a new pronounced round dent, approximately two-and one-half inches in diameter. I looked closer and realized the dent had some small markings around its edge. It then dawned on me that the van had been hit with possibly a beer, or soda bottle's bottom end. The small markings resembled those often embossed around the bottom of glass bottles. The bottle had most likely been thrown out from a passing car traveling northbound. The bottle had hit my van's front end, bottom first. I then looked closer and determined the dent was just below my VW bus windshield's bottom edge.

Had I been driving any normal height sedan the bottle would have hit the windshield. Both the windshield and bottle would have shattered and then smashed directly into my face at high speed. It could have killed me. Now madder than hell, I wanted to chase the car down and beat someone's stupid ass. My VW bus didn't have enough speed for a chase and I didn't see the color, make or model of the northbound vehicle. Still fuming, I continued on my way south. I was still cussing and mad enough to do some real body damage to some stupid ass on the highway!

13. *When I worked thirty years carrying a gun on the job.* I was around twenty-three years old to twenty-six. [From age twenty-six to thirty I was in college.] Then, from age thirty-two, to age fifty-five; that's a span of thirty years I had worked in law enforcement. I spent seven years as a street cop working in three cities, one in

Missouri and two In California. I spent twenty-three years as a Deputy Marshal working in the California court system. I made hundreds of car stops, worked a lot of accident scenes, and arrested hundreds of people for various crimes. I never fired my gun while on duty. I had my gun drawn on three occasions and decided it wasn't necessary to shoot a person. I retired after thirty years, uninjured. I had survived.

Summary: Now as a retiree, I can write about my life experiences. Those things I encountered while growing up, serving in the navy, attending college and for the years I had worked in law enforcement.

We Got a Need to Be Free

by Phil Silverman

I got a need to be free
Wanderlust gets the best of us, best of me
It's really nice to be married
But I sometimes need to nurse a slurpee
At 2:30
In the morning

I leave my wife back in bed
After we interlock and I massage her head
I feel something strong coming on
But sometimes I need to read an LA Times
opinion
At 7:30
in the evening

A good job and a pad
The best friends a guy ever had
A big mahogany desk
Eager intern in a short tight dress;
Come and go as I please
Make my monthly goal - then I ride the breeze
Ah...such sweet memories!
(Except for my mutton chops and crooked 'stach and that
Buick Skyhawk with the rattling flywheel-helluva heater,
though)

Hey, the Founding Mothers
Said to the Fathers
Cut me loose, baby
You gave us a free country!
Our apartment complex
needs extra security
so work the Welcome desk on Saturdays
- you see, we need our weekly Walmart spree

The Native and African Americans
Told those Know it alls
You wrote a good creed
about life and
Liberty
But
Set me free
Let me control my OWN destiny.

Charlie O'Brien, Private Investigator

By Professor Alan Dale Dickinson

Some people say that *our* man, Charlie, has the sharp eye of a falcon, or an *eagle* (like *Swoop* the Philadelphia Eagle NFL mascot or the toughness of the LA Ram NFL mascot), and a truer aim with a pistol or an automatic rifle than you will ever find.

They always add that old Charlie is a devoted and long-time follower of his personal *Mantra.* That is to say in Charlie's own words, "A person should do what they say that they are going to do, but, if they do not do what they promise that they will do, then, they should be held accountable for their wrongful actions."

Also, they say that he was very well thought of by the Police, the CIA, and his fellow private detectives. They go on to add that he never asked them to do anything that he would not do himself, nothing at all.

The people in this very dangerous, line of work, law enforcement, et cetera, notice things like that, they truly do. Charlie, they said, was always the first man 'through the door' of the bad guy's locations.

And was the first person to get shot at or even take a bullet. Most of these former, and present, associates of his always did their best to support him and watch his back whenever they went into battle (got into a gun firefight).

He had been in many quite dangerous, precarious and life-threatening situations with Howard from the CIA, John from the FBI, the LAPD Police Chief, Charlie (another good guy named, Charlie), amongst many, many other detectives *and* Private Eyes and even some famed Navy Seals.

All of them down to the very last one, said that Charlie was such a good role model of the 'good guys' that they would always do their utmost for him and even give up their lives for him if necessary. They said, he was the first to come to the aid of another agent or operative who was in trouble or wounded on a *dangerous* mission.

And that he was one of the bravest people they had ever worked or served with.

All of them, said that they would follow Charlie anywhere, anytime, and any place, and they sounded like they meant it, they really did. He always encouraged the new recruits, new agents, and operatives, always.

Now, if you were to ask Charlie about these 'glowing' and very generous compliments, he would tell you and me that they are not true or that they were overrated.

And that the men and women who made such very gracious comments about him were the real *"heroes"* and not him. Charlie is actually a modest guy, albeit, you would never guess that by the way he carries himself while on the job.

Also, he would add to that statement, that those kind people were just as brave and courageous as he was, and probably even more so. Well, definitely more so, he would add.

Charlie has been shot, as well as stabbed, several times over the years while exercising his very dangerous and risky vocation as a private investigator. He puts on his body 'armor' as he goes amongst the *demons* in *this world.'*

That is to say, that by being a LAPD 'Robbery and Homicide' Detective, a covert operative for the CIA and the FBI, the NSA, the OCSD, and working on quite death-defying cases involving some of the most evil and hardened criminals in the world he needs and uses bullet-proof vests, guns, knives and protection and body armor.

And he always adds a true, however very odd sounding comment, he says that he does not mind being wounded nor hurt "on-the-job". That is a little bit of a funny statement don't you think? In addition, he says that the way he looks at it, getting injured is just an occupational hazard, that's all it is. Very similar to a construction worker losing a finger, or his big toe; or a firefighter (fireman and/or firewoman) getting burned in a raging fire while rescuing men, women, children, and their beloved pets from certain death.

It's an occupational hazard not unlike a doctor or nurse who catches a serious (and sometimes even deadly) illness from a very sick patient; Or people who work in factories and foundries, who lose arms, legs, and or their lives.

Or consider a banker who gets shot or stabbed during a bank 'hold-up', or placed and locked in the bank vault without any ventilation. Or any number of other vocations (and there are more than you think) that carry with them the risk of injury or death.

Funny, but the only thing that Charlie ever complains about is not being hurt at the office (kidding). The times in the hospital critical care centers or the long recovery time when he gets home irritate him, that's all.

He hates that the most, he says. And he cannot wait to get back 'on the streets' to investigate and then solve some more heinous 'White Collar' crimes somewhere in this crazy, mixed-up world of ours. Just anywhere on the globe is fine with him.

Just like the fearless moderator, John Walsh, of 'America's Most Wanted' real life TV show, (it was on Fox Network for years, but now is on CNN), Charlie wants to be out there 'looking for the bad guys'. Charlie said he believes that John is just an incredible person.

John and Charlie both say, "Here in the good ole US of A, as well as all over the entire world they will hunt their evil prey." Both of them have traveled thousands of miles around the globe searching for, and locating, evil crooks and criminals. They truly have.

Absolutely nothing in this world makes Charlie happier than when he locates, arrests, and sees them convicted in a court of law. It makes him ecstatic it really does.

And then after that, to see them put in captivity in a dark hole somewhere. And he always adds, "preferably in a horrible and deplorable 'third-world' prison.

Dios will mete out justice of the severest kind imaginable to those who do despicable things to women and children, as well as the elderly and the defenseless.

Charlie loves to teach. He used to teach law enforcement classes at both Cal State University and Fullerton Community College in Fullerton, California at one time.

He still holds a Life-Time Teaching Credential from the Department of Education in Sacramento, California. And when he semi-retires from being a *Private Eye*, he is planning on going back to teaching at Saddleback Community College in the Orange County or Cal-State University-Fullerton, soon.

Charlie is a big strong and very tough guy, but he is also very gracious and caring at the same time. And he always laughs when he hears someone say, "Here he comes, our man, Charlie Brown," and gives them a big old smile too.

In real life, Charlie's Lucy is his lovely wife Lynn. Lucy in the cartoon is cute, albeit, his *Philly* girl looks just like a model, she truly does. Also, more importantly, much more importantly, she is an absolutely incredible woman with the graciousness of the women of olden days.

Charlie and Sarge

By Professor Alan Dale Dickinson

Charlie, Sarge and the new Undersheriff *Robert (Bob) Peterson* rolled up to a co-op (similar to a Condo) located at number 666 Calle Aragon in lovely LWV (Laguna Woods Village). The undersheriff joined them at Sarge's request.

The undersheriff works directly under the great Orange County Sheriff and Chief Coroner, *Don Barnes* and also is second in command of the entire OCSD (Orange County Sheriff's Department).

Charlie and Sarge wanted Bob to get a first-hand look at the beautiful community that all of a sudden, after 60 years, is having a rash of 'shootings' for some strange and unknown reason.

By the way, Sarge told Charlie, "Bob is very well thought of by all of the rank and file OCSD personnel. Also, he is a career Law Enforcement officer and has been quite successful at every post that he has served on."

Charlie said to Sarge and Bob, "I don't like this address number '666', not one little bit. It gives me the creeps, it really does." Earlier Sarge had got a call from OCSD Dispatch in Santa Ana that someone at this address was brandishing a weapon.

The Dispatch Officer said that he was afraid that there may be another 'shooting' in Laguna Woods Village. And that there had been several lately out there. Right after that earlier call, Charlie, Sarge, and Bob were on the scene in less than 60 seconds.

Even from the outside, the co-op at number '666' looked 'dark and foreboding' to the three investigators. Charlie said to the other two men, "It looks like death to me, for some reason."

Then he added, "Sarge, you and Bob watch your backs." Charlie noticed that it was very quiet, eerily quiet, in other words, way, way too quiet for Charlie's taste.

They started to carefully, very carefully, walk up to the front door. Then Charlie, said to Bob, "Can you cover the rear for us?" And Bob immediately, faster than a speeding bullet, had his 40

Caliber Glock automatic pistol drawn from his custom-made leather shoulder holster (that he bought on one of his shopping trips to Tijuana, Mexico) in his right hand and also a .357 Smith and Wesson revolver in his left hand.

The undersheriff had worked in some very *rough* areas 'back in the day' and he knew how to *get* down when he had too. Sarge pulled out his .45 Caliber auto with a 15 round ammo clip.

Charlie removed his .44 Magnum Smith and Wesson (the Clint Eastwood Dirty Harry gun of choice). Also, he had a Marine K-Bar knife in his belt, in case of any hand-to- hand combat with whoever was in there.

Just as Charlie and Sarge got to the front door, Charlie heard a little click, which to his keen ear, sounded just like a *shotgun* hammer being pulled back.

Then 30 seconds later, just a heartbeat so to speak, Charlie and Sarge, heard a 'shotgun' blast which went bam, bam. That meant that it was a double-barreled shotgun and the perp fired both barrels in very rapid succession.

One second earlier and both of them would have been 'toast,' if you know what I mean. But Charlie had just thrown Sarge into the planter full of soft bushes just to the right of the front door with the madman behind it with his old faithful shotgun.

They landed right under the address on the side of the co-op, which when they both looked up showed the spooky address, '666'. Charlie felt a shiver go up his spine while he was hiding in the little planter with Sarge.

Some of the shotgun *pellets* hit Charlie in his upper left shoulder and arm and a few hit his big thick neck. Sarge was shot also, he was hit in his left arm and his back.

Thank Abba, neither were wounded very badly, but another trip to the ER at the wonderful St. Jude Medical Center in Fullerton, California with the great and caring Dr. Anne was still in order.

Charlie found out from a local real estate agent, that the co-op at 666 Calle Aragon in Laguna Woods Village is always either vacant and/ or for sale. And it has been that way for the past 55 years.

Charlie said to Sarge, "Not hard to figure that one out old man. That number is bad mojo or bad karma or both, if you know what I mean." Sarge just nodded his head because he knew exactly what Charlie was saying.

Then he replied after a few moments, "Sarge, do you think that the number 666 has some Biblical reference in this case and at this residence?" Charlie responded what the nice and very sharp real estate lady had said to him, "Yes, Charlie perhaps it does, if you believe in that sort of thing?"

Charlie said to the realtor, "Yes, actually I do believe in that sort of thing. I think that the reason why I am still alive and kicking today, is because of that sort of thing."

After Charlie got up from being shot with the shotgun blast, one blast had hit him and the other blast had hit Sarge, he got mad, real mad, and then he got even madder.

He yelled at Sarge, "I am sick and tired of being shot at for no good reason." Then he kicked open the front door of the co-op which now had a gaping hole right in the middle of it from the two shotgun blasts.

The low-down-dirty shotgun-shooter, as it turns out, was a highly bi-polar former Entertainment Director for the property management company LMS, Inc. (Laguna Woods Management Services, Inc.).

He was a tall man, about 6'4" and around 69 years old. And he was a little bit unstable, well a lot unstable, when off of his meds, according to Charlie.

Later on, the shooter said that he thought that Charlie and Sarge were Russian FSB (formerly KGB) agents. Charlie asked Sarge, "Do you think that we look like foreign Russian agents?"

Sarge quickly replied, "I don't think I do, but I think that you do Charlie." And then he had a big belly laugh and added, "Just kidding Charlie, you don't really look like a KGB Ruskey."

Then Sarge laughed even louder, and said, "Alright, no, you don't look like a Russian, but you do look like a very suspicious character." And laughed some more. Charlie said to him, "I am so happy that you have me to make fun of, someone else might be offended by your silly jokes".

Charlie and Sarge love to tease each other even though they are best of friends. Just like Crockett and Tubbs in the hit 1984 *Miami Vice* TV show. Charlie thinks that he gets the best of Sarge in their battering back and forth.

While Sarge thinks that he comes out on top most of the time. It's probably a 'toss-up' if you ask me. Charlie wins half of the time and Sarge wins the other half.

Later, the *undersheriff* put the shotgun kid in the back of his 'black and white' Chevy Tahoe SUV, which had a big block 'police interceptor' 454 c.i. V-8 engine, and swished the shooter off to the OCSD Leo Lacy Jail.

Charlie told Sarge that he was very glad that the Bob had been with them at the shooting, also for his help in getting rid of the criminal so quickly. The perp will face some serious time for attempting to kill an OCSD deputy as well as a civilian. Unless they send him to the mental ward at UCI (University of Irvine Medical Center), of course.

So, Charlie said, "It's sad, but ole number '666' is once again up for sale. The neighbors forced the estate and the relatives of the shooter to sell it. They wanted to get a new neighbor, one who does not wave a shotgun in their faces."

"I wonder," Charlie to Sarge, "Do you know anybody who is interested in buying a haunted house?" Sarge spit back, very quickly, "No Charlie I don't and certainly I would not want to live at that 666 (mark of the *beast*) address."

Then he added, "I would, however, love to live in lovely Laguna Woods Village someday when I get old *like* you Charlie." Charlie's response, "Funny Sarge, very, very, funny."

Later on, Sarge said that it was, "he who shoved Charlie to the ground thus saving his life and not the 'other' way around. You know our man Charlie he tends to exaggerate a little bit (or a lot) every now and then."

YIMBY (Yes in My Backyard)
By Suellen Zima

Picture this—a piece of cardboard on the ground and a person sleeping on it. The caption reads, "This bed costs $100,759 a year." No, this is not a far-away third world country. This is Southern California, Orange County.

The happy hobo image of homelessness doesn't exist. In Orange County, California, one of the richest counties in our country, the face of homelessness is wrinkled, old and weak. At last count, made one night in 2019, there were 455 homeless seniors found and interviewed. Yes, there were also other categories of homeless people found and interviewed. But there were more homeless seniors interviewed that night compared to every other category.

I learned at a United Way Homelessness 101 lecture on homelessness in Orange County, that the cure for homelessness is putting people in homes. And by every comparison, the cost is by far cheaper than the $100,750 spent on each homeless person for the many services they use when they are homeless.

While non-homeless people have the wrong notion that the homeless in Orange County are recent arrivals because of the warm climate, the average person found in that one-night survey had been a resident of Orange County for about ten years.

There is a tornado of circumstances swirling in Orange County. Even a large percentage of working people can no longer afford to live here because the prices of buying and renting are way beyond normal, or even good salaries. Along with rising life expectancy into the 80's, 90's and 100's that can affect income, there is a scarcity of housing in the county in general and especially for low incomes. Plus, other expenses are rising beyond an older person's capacity to increase income.

After my mother died, my father and I moved to a retirement community then called Leisure World in Southern California. Neither my dad nor I had enough money to buy our home, so we pooled our resources and bought a two-bedroom home for $73,500. At that time, the range of prices for homes here was perhaps $60,000 to $600,000. But the shared cost concept with a monthly fee allowed all who lived here to share in the clubhouses, a tempting variety of amenities, classes, and over 200 resident-run clubs.

During the twenty years since that time, my dad died, house prices went up and up, and then drastically down and down in 2008, and modestly up again. And the required monthly fee also increased regularly. Now you can still buy a one-bedroom home in the Village for perhaps $155,000, but there are many more homes now above one million dollars.

If you can't continue to pay the mortgage or the monthly fee, you are eventually forced to leave the Village. And go where? Certainly not anywhere else in all of Orange County, and most of California. You can become a statistic of homelessness and some do. And, as I'm finding out, more and more of my aging neighbors are running out of money and fear homelessness. It's a heavy burden of worry. I know, I'm one of them.

I searched for help and found California YIMBY. It empowers citizens in advocating for affordable housing and countering NIMBY (Not in My Backyard) efforts that seek to disrupt and prevent housing progress.

After the Fire

By Jerry Schur

Sandy steered his Jeep along the rubble-strewn street and stopped at 1301 Oaktree Lane, or what used to be 1301. Now only the cement slab remained, blanketed in debris. The only part of the house still standing was the fireplace chimney, its stone presence towering over the wasteland like a sentinel after a battle. The sight of ashes brought back the acrid odor of the smoke.

One chapter of his life had started and ended here, so what better place to flip back the pages of his life and decide his future? He had been up all night thinking about what to do, but couldn't reach a decision. He'd thought he was content, sliding along, satisfied with his life, and then, bam. An ultimatum.

Fourteen years ago, after a heart attack, he had retired from his restaurant at age forty-five. He and Debbie moved here for the blue California skies and the eternal beauty of the wooded mountains. Back then houses stood all around, and the view was breathtaking. Now, two years after the fire, and a drought, the mountains were no longer green, but dusty brown. The fire had steamrollered the houses. Rubble still dominated everywhere, though he noticed the Andersons on the next street had erected a house frame. Rebuilding. Good luck to them.

Sandy swung in his seat, slid his six-foot frame out of the Jeep feet first and walked through the ashes to where their patio had been. Many an evening he and Debbie had sat there sipping white wine. If they had bickered during the day, it often stopped then.

They had searched here after the fire, at first finding a few things worth saving, but none lately. Today he saw again the remains of their bed, only part of a metal leg, charred and melted. His boot toe moved a bent strip of metal, once a picture frame. What picture did it hold? Who could tell?

The fire had gobbled up objects: his high school yearbook, pictures of his fraternity brothers, and of his sister's kids growing up. Also lost letters from his parents long gone, some favorite books, the first dollar he'd ever earned at his restaurant. And of course, wedding pictures, the honeymoon in Greece, their vacations in China and Australia, all gone.

As he moseyed about, moving the ashes with his foot, he found a four-inch shard of yellow ceramic. He picked it up, scraped off the dirt and put it in his jacket pocket. It was part of a vase, a wedding present from Debbie's aunt. It had been a stunning piece, four feet tall, blazing yellow and orange, commissioned from a prominent local artist. Now the vase was gone, and so was the marriage, both victims of the fire.

Debbie never recovered from the loss. They had bickered before, but after the fire there were heated arguments, followed by cold hours of no communication. Debbie drank a lot. Smoldering grievances flared up into flaming disputes. Sandy thought it was mostly her fault, but that didn't matter.

When she left, he didn't have the will to stop her. There was a quick divorce. He thought he'd never see her again.

A year after the fire he'd met Jen. Thinking about her had kept him awake all night.

He first saw her in a karaoke bar where she sang loudly and a bit off key, but clearly, she relished life. Her long blond hair and broad smile beckoned him. They talked. She owned a beauty salon with six chairs. Divorced, her only son was a CPA in Chicago.

They began to see each other. They both liked Johnny Cash and Billie Holiday. She suggested trips to the Queen Mary and Disneyland where he pranced under a Mickey Mouse hat. Later they had a weekend in Cabo. He liked the way she touched his arm when they were together. For months he floated along, passive and content.

Once he visited her salon and admired her no nonsense directing of the beauticians. She had an iron fist in a velvet glove. Then, a week ago, Debbie popped up out of his past. He had thought she was history, but she wanted to see him. At first, he thought no, but he couldn't wipe out a dozen years of his life. She told him, "I know I just flipped out. You were right to get a divorce, but I've been through therapy. I've seen a shrink twice a week for a year, and stopped drinking. I'm fine now and I want to see you, to hear all about you."

They drove down to the ocean for lunch at a restaurant perched above the water. She was the old Debbie, at her best, smiling and happy. They strolled through a sidewalk art show, looking at landscapes and paintings of boats. When he saw her to her car she hugged him. "It was wonderful being with you."

"Yes, it was great to see you again," he said and meant it.

"We must do this again soon."

He didn't know what to say, so he mumbled, "Yes." She had suddenly pushed back into his life, an unexpected complication.

He didn't tell Jen. Two days later for Jen's fiftieth birthday, they had dinner at an Italian restaurant, her favorite. They sat side by side in a red leather booth. Pictures of Rome, Venice and Naples adorned the walls. He gave her a present, a pearl necklace. She seemed disappointed.

Her fork poked at the steaming spaghetti arrabiata. She looked up and said, "It's interesting you always order the same thing here, rotini pomodoro."

"Yes, and you always order something different, as if you're searching for the perfect taste."

"Not perfect, just better."

Sandy speared some pasta with his fork. They were both silent.

"You know I love you," she said.

"And I love you. I've told you that many times. We've been together almost every night since we met. What has it been? Four months?"

"Five months, two weeks, and three days." She pursed her lips. "Everything's been so good. "Just being together, at karaoke or sitting on your couch holding hands and watching the Big Bang Theory."

He broke a piece of bread off the loaf and chewed.

"Honey," she said, "we've danced around this for a while. What is our future?"

Sandy was uncomfortable. He knew what she wanted, but he wasn't sure what he wanted.

Jen put her hand on his. "I've thought about us for a long time. I don't think we should go on like this. It's not fair for either of us. We should decide to get married, or... I think we should break it off."

This was like a car crash. He had vaguely suspected this moment might come, but not so soon. He was silent.

"We're not teen-agers. Being divorced has taught us what marriage is. I know what I'm looking for, you. I want to spend the rest of my life with you, and if you can't make that commitment..."

He put down his fork. He had no appetite.

"My sister lived with a guy for six years," she said. "Then he up and left. I promised myself that wouldn't happen to me. Let's set a timetable. One week. I told you I'm going to visit my son in Chicago then. I'm either going to tell him we're getting married or that we're done. Think about it," she said. "I know it's the best thing for me and for you too, but you have to decide. I must move on, hopefully with you, or maybe not." Her eyes were moist. His heart was jumping.

As Sandy walked over the missing walls, he bit his cheek, wishing for a cigarette, but his smoking days were long gone. Looking down at the ashes, he knew they were his past. Debbie was his past. He wouldn't go down that road again. He took the yellow shard from his pocket and tossed it on the rubble. Now Jen wanted him to start over. If he did, would it end in disaster? He looked where the Anderson house was going up. Anderson was his age, choosing to build a new future. That was right for him too, with Jen.

"I've always been an optimist," he thought. His heart warmed with his decision. He was anxious to see Jen. He'd call her as soon as he was past the winding roads. As he climbed into the Jeep, he glanced down at a yellow wildflower pushing its head out of the ashes.

A Tree Grows in Brooklyn
A Book Review
By Allan Rankin

If you are to read only one book in a lifetime, it should be *A Tree Grows in Brooklyn* by Betty Smith. This is a highly symbolic title for a book that relies on truth and harsh reality to convey a touching story of a young girl's early childhood. It is a story set in the tenement district of Brooklyn, where foreigners struggle against the brutality of poverty. Like the tree that grew in Brooklyn's empty lots, rubbish heaps, and even out of the sidewalks, Francie Nolan "struggled to reach the sky." More than a book about life, from its worst elements to its finest, it is a book about literacy, imagination, courage, and honesty.

In short, it is a book about power—spiritual power.

The children in *A Tree Grows in Brooklyn*, at least the ones who survive, assimilate and perpetuate the brawling insensitivity that characterized early twentieth century living. But not Francie Nolan; she saw the cycle clearly and unlike the babies who came into the world like, "an accordion pulled out full for a rich note, then closing...closing... closing from beautiful baby to old age and death," she vowed to rise up.

Francie was introduced early to Shakespeare, and the "Bible that the Protestant people read," She loved her little old shabby library and said, "it was as good as the feeling she had for church." With her love for books she overcame the poverty, isolation and insensitivity of the streets. She also learned about hard work, truth and frugality, symbolized by the tin-can bank nailed down in the closet, where she learned the value of saving. The bank was a small, but powerful bridge between poverty and prosperity, even slavery and freedom, on the road to becoming a property owner.

In her grandmother's words, "Once one has owned land, there is no going back to being a serf."

Life was hard, and typical of the times was the treatment neighborhood women rendered Joanna, a young neighbor girl, while airing her out-of-wedlock baby in its carriage. Beaten down and miserable in their own lives, the women chided, cursed and threw stones at Joanna just for being there. Even Francie declined to return her smile because her mother had warned her, "Let Joanna be a lesson for *you*." The lesson she learned, though, was "she hated those women, she feared them for their devious ways, she mistrusted their instincts." Most importantly she learned to hate intolerance.

Francie gave Joanna and her baby her first published essay; the first thing in her life she was proud of. The essay was a symbol of her identity, and precious to her, but her parents were never to see it. It filled her in the same way the child filled Joanna. But, feeling like an accomplice to the intolerance that denied Joanna that pride, Francie also denied herself the adoration and praise from her parents.

Brooklyn at that time even added a cruel twist to the custom of selling Christmas trees. The word on the street was if someone waited until the end, "They'd chuck 'em at you." But both Francie and her brother were too small to carry the tree. You have to admire her courage when she argues with the tree man, and says, "me and my brother—we're not too little together." When he threw the tree at them, they took it with all its force. Bloodied but smiling they heard the man say, "and now get the hell out of here with your tree, you lousy bastards."

Francie had heard swearing all her life and she knew it to be "the emotional expressions of inarticulate people with small vocabularies." In the same way the tree that symbolizes Christmas was forcefully thrown at her, she knew he was really saying, "Goodbye—God bless you."

A Tree Grows in Brooklyn is a powerful message for all who have the courage, no matter how poor, to fight for their birthright. Francie Nolan starts life as a sickly child with little hope of surviving. With the ugly streets, drunks, rapists, crooked politicians, mean schools and bad teachers, who would ever expect her to go to University?

Betty Smith, the author, weaves her characters in and out of this rich setting, highlighted by the images of music, childbirth, life and death. Like the tree that some in Brooklyn called, "The Tree of Heaven," the children grew to be strong because the hard struggle to live made them strong. As Betty Smith says, "This tree that men chopped down…this tree that they built a bonfire around, trying to burn up its stump—this tree lived!"

This tree was Francie Nolan in *A Tree Grows in Brooklyn.*

Deadly Rope

By Jill Amadio

They found his body two days before the Big Game. Swinging gently in the wind that swept lazily across the prairie on a sunny Thursday morning, he was hanging from a rope looped over the lowest branch of the tall tree. The lone live oak was a landmark visible for miles from the low-lying ranchlands and the Papago Indian reservation that reached to the horizon.

"Who is it? Can ya see?" yelled the two cattle hands to each other as they urged their horses to a faster gallop. "One of them migrants that got through the border fence? I told Dawson the barbed wire was too easy to cut."

"Could be. Maybe a lynching like that one in Nogales last year. Oh, God! It's that kid, Sonny Devlin!"

It wasn't difficult to bring the skinny teenager down, I learned from them later. One rider stayed in his saddle to reach up and slice through the rope while the other dismounted to catch the body as it was released. They laid him gently down on the grass.

"Dang! Look at that. He used his favorite bull riding rope. Looks like the special braided one he earned the championship with at the Four Corners rodeo. Made it himself."

"Too bad. The kid sure had lots of try, but he won't make the national college rodeo finals team now. Nor the Big Game. Here's where he climbed up the trunk. See those marks? Guess we should get the sheriff out here."

In our small town of three hundred close to the Arizona-Mexico border where you either worked on a ranch or labored in the fields now that the copper mines were closed, the death of anyone was mourned by all of us. In this case the death of Sonny, our star junior varsity soccer player and rodeo contestant, was a sensation in a community that despite its small size was often at odds with itself.

Any event out of the ordinary and people quickly took sides. Rumors would swirl and everyone argued, but mostly it was peaceful and quiet. I heard the news about my friend's suicide on our local radio station KDXL while I was driving home from my new summer job with one of the tourist outfits that guided visiting fishermen at Crumb State Park Lake. I was so shocked by the news I stomped on the gas and pushed the Ram to 95.

Sonny and I were in the same graduating class at Riddock High School and on the soccer team. I parked more crooked than usual at home, even though it always drove Mom wiggy, and ran inside. She was reading the Holy Bible, so I didn't bother her. Out the window, miles away, I watched the sun setting on the O'Reilly ranch house. It was the only really large house in our area and set on their thousand or so acres outside of town. The O'Reillys were the richest ranching family around. The rest of us lived in trailers or real small homes that were mostly shacks built for miners back in the 1800s.

There was nothing much for kids to do except play sports and our schools responded to our needs with basketball, soccer, football, and rodeo teams. Until I was twelve years old, me and Mom went to church on Sundays and I'd have to stay after the service to attend Sunday School.

After Sonny got his driver's license, he'd drive me and Robert into Ajo, the next town over, to hang out, but with hardly any money, the most entertainment we could find was to stroll through the penny arcade. Or we'd sit outside the cowboy bar dipping Copenhagen tobacco we'd snitched from the five and dime and listen to the country music blaring out from the bar, scrambling out the way when a drunk was thrown through the swinging saloon doors.

We'd smoke skanky low-grade pot, too, while my friends planned pranks to play on our classmates and teachers. Some of their suggestions weren't that funny or pleasant and some sounded cruel. I never participated in their tricks, especially when their ideas got wilder and wilder, which made me wonder why Sonny and Robert let me hang around. I was known as a loner, a real quiet guy with basically no other friends. I knew they figured me for kind of a jerk, but I didn't really care. I felt sort of privileged to be their buddy because they were both on the basketball team as well as the soccer team. I'd tried out for basketball but never got picked.

Sonny and Robert lived next door to each other and were always visiting, but our trailer was a mile east at the other end of town. Mom kept a close eye on me ever since Dad died in an accident floating logs down the river for the sawmill he worked at in Montana after the mine here closed. I never told Mom about driving to Ajo. I knew she'd never let me go if I asked her permission. Instead, I said I'd be watching the rodeo practice. It was a white lie, I knew that, but I decided it would save her some anxiety and that God would forgive me. Besides, I'd be eighteen in three months and be my own person.

I wanted to know how Robert was handling the suicide. Had Sonny left a note for his parents? Why would he hang himself? I walked down to Robert's place instead of driving in order to save on gas as usual and saw Sheriff Townsend's truck outside. Looked like the sheriff was asking some questions. I didn't go in. I didn't need to. I sat near the tall cactus beneath the open living room window as I sometimes did when Sonny and Robert didn't want me around. I listened to their secrets but never let on.

"You mean to tell me," I heard the sheriff say, "Sonny Devlin never gave you any indication he wanted to take his life? You were close friends, right?"

"Yes sir. But I had no idea he'd really do it."

"Do it? Kill himself? What are you talking about?" The sheriff's deep voice rose to a shout and I could imagine his big beer belly quivering. He hated any kind of crime in his territory, but this was a different situation. "You knew what he was going to do?"

"Well, Sonny and I had this pact, sir. We were kind of tired of livin' here 'cos there's never anything goin' on." Robert's tone turned whiny. "None of the girls would date us because they said we were goofy and mean. So Sonny and I agreed that if things didn't change by the end of the month we'd just put an end to our misery. It was just a joke on ourselves. I never thought he was serious, sir."

"You stupid kids. You don't know what misery is. A joke on yourselves? Ever think about your parents? You're sick."

I heard the sheriff stomp out, slamming the screen door, and I scurried around the side of the house to hide. After his truck pulled away, I went to the front and called out. Robert's mom appeared. She wore the same stained green apron I always saw her in tied loosely around her thick body. Sometimes she'd forget she was wearing it and come to school with it on.

Her face was pale and tear tracks marked her cheeks

"Sam, come on in. Sure is a sad, sad day. Want a soda?"

"No, ma'am, thank you. I just came round to see how Robert is."

I looked at my friend sitting on the sofa, his spindly legs sprawled over the faded blue cushions, and wondered why he didn't seem upset.

"Hey, Sam, I got something to show you," he said, getting up. "Let's go outside."

He wanted to walk a little ways off from the house. Then he stopped, bent down and pulled something from his boot. He gave it to me. Written on a piece of lined paper, the same as in our spiral exercise notebooks for school, were the words, "We, Sonny and Robert, promise each other to commit suicide if neither of us gets a kiss from Jenny Slater by the end of this month."

I saw both their signatures. At the bottom was the date, July 31. Sonny had waited only one day before actually carrying out the silliest threat I'd ever heard of and stringing himself up.
"Jeez, another one of your childish stunts," I said, handing the paper back to him. "Except this time, it's a tragedy and real, real dumb. You ever going to grow up, dude?"

Robert flicked back the hank of blond hair that always fell across his forehead and smirked.

"Well, the joke's on Sonny. I ain't gonna kill myself like him, Sam. He was nuts to believe I really would."

"But, Robert, he kept his side of the bargain. Now you're betraying him. You signed the note."

"What? Are you serious?" He scowled at me with that weird thing he always did with his mouth when he didn't like something. "I told you, no way am I gonna do it. You're crazy."

My parents brought me up as a good, God-fearing Christian although I rarely attended church anymore. I knew the Ten Commandants and parts of the Bible from Sunday School where we'd often been reminded that our word was sacred and that we had to honor our pledges. I sighed and shrugged my shoulders.

"Hey, there's Sonny's truck over there." I said. "Let's go sit in it as sort of like a mark of respect."

We walked over to the dusty black pickup that Sonny's Dad had given him on his 16th birthday. It was bigger than anyone else had in Riddock, a crew cab with four doors instead of two and room for extra people in back.

"Sit in the driver's seat," I told Robert. I walked around to the passenger side but instead of getting into the front I opened the rear door and stepped up, sitting behind Robert to give him what I figured was some private space, the kind folks need for grieving. There wasn't a lot of room on the back bench seat for my chunky frame because some of Sonny's gear for soccer and rodeo was spread around. I asked Robert if he felt close to Sonny's spirit.

"Maybe we should say a prayer," I said.

"A prayer?" Robert's laugh was loud, long, and mocking.

As I shifted on the seat in dismay and embarrassment at his reaction my left hand fell upon the rope reins that Sonny used when he practiced bronc riding. He was never any good at it, nothing like with his bull riding, but the dude'd kept on trying.

The rope reins were made of good quality sisal in a nice beige color when his Dad first bought them but with use, they'd turned a dirty dark brown. I was always wanting to try them out on Sonny's horse, but Sonny sneered when I asked, pointing out I wasn't a rodeo rider and wouldn't know what to do. He was right about that, but I still wanted to know what rope reins felt like in my hands. They were standard size, 7 ft. in length. Plenty long enough. I picked them up, wrapped an end around each hand and threw the center part over Robert's head in front of me, pulling Sonny's rope reins tight around his neck.

After Robert stopped struggling I realized I had found exactly the right meaning for a word I'd learned recently in class but figured I'd never, ever have any use for: ironic. And how fitting that I was kinda helping Robert honor his pledge and keep his word. Just like we'd been taught in Sunday school. I knew Mom would be real proud of me.

Cutting Up with Sunshine

By Sunshine Lutey

I live with Sunshine; I met her in 2004. She and her sister Waverly enthusiastically rummaged the shops to supply Sunshine's new Colorado home with beautiful furnishings. My cousins and I lived with her for four months before we moved back to her Mariposa home in Laguna Woods Village, California. Today we share her San Amadeo home in Laguna Woods Village.

I'm a glass cutting board and I contain a beautiful picture of a lighthouse on top of a rocky ledge where ocean waves crash against the rocky shore below. Smoke rises from two chimneys and light shines from within the pictured buildings. I was gorgeous. I heard Sunshine say so.

My eight cousins are glass coasters with the identical scene. Today they still grace Sunshine's tables.

A month ago, I nearly lost my life. Through the years, the beautiful picture inside me suffered damage so I lost some of my beauty. With sadness in my heart, I watched and listened as Sunshine tried to find a replacement for me; to my utter joy, she was not successful.

One day I saw her open a package and heard her exclaim happily, "Oh, you are lovely!" She held a new glass cutting board with an embedded picture of Victoria Falls. I have to admit it looked great; I couldn't help the jealousy and fear that coursed through me.

She laid me aside and placed her new purchase in my spot; I was dying inside and knew my life with Sunshine was almost over. Then it happened; it was unthinkably wonderful. She looked at me lovingly and said, "I won't give you up."

Now her kitchen has two beautiful cutting boards. Yes, I lost some of my beauty but I'm no longer jealous. I'm proud and happy to grace one of Sunshine's countertops.

Leftover

By Phil Silverman

I'm just a leftover from a seven-course meal
at a fabuleux Français restaurant
"Un carafe d'eau s'il vous plaît"
And "le chèque" while you're on your way
Il est pour le divertissement, they will say!
Then I shove my escargots in my handy zip lock
I stay nice and warm while waiting at the dock and watching that
big old clock where the three corners meet on le boulevard.

They don't do boxes at such a place
Never ask at all or you could
get maced!

Know that I'm freezable up to four months
and can't possibly rot
I'm cold right now but soon
I'll be Luke hot
Don't heat me with veggies in an old crock pot
You'll kill the essence of my coalescence
more often than not!

Finally, may I boldly suggest with no jest, just some gastronomic
zest -
Try me with Angel Hair!
Just add butter with care!
And Sea salt makes
me crunchy and delectable, funky food fare.

The Dutchman

By Jon Perkins

'Pappy' Whitlock brushed long gray strands of hair that were obscuring his left eye and tucked them behind his ear. He stood stock still and looked down at the ground around his scuffed brown boots and listened. The sound was unmistakable and not all that unusual, the rattle of an angry snake less than a yard from his feet. Standing still was no guarantee that the snake wouldn't go ahead and strike anyway. It was March, when the snakes come out of hibernation and shed their skins. Hundreds of them. Hell, maybe thousands. They were everywhere, hungry and mean.

When rattlesnakes shed their skins, they go blind and have to rely on their heat sensors, pits on either side of their head that detect infrared radiation and provide an image of a living target. Pappy had years of experience with rattlesnakes, which was the reason for the loss of two fingers on his left hand and a bunch of scars where he'd cut deep to drain off the venom. It was also the reason why the six chambers of his Ruger Blackhawk were now loaded for snakes, a bunch of small lead BBs packed into cartridges. Without making sudden movements that might provoke the snake into action, he removed the weapon from the holster on his right hip. The snake was camouflaged in the tangle of a Baja Ruellia bush that had just turned color with purple buds. He could have just edged away and there wouldn't have been a problem. Snakes were important foragers for pests in the Arizona desert, feeding on rats and mice and other small animals.

Pappy didn't care. He hated snakes. He cocked the single-action .44 revolver and blasted the bush and whatever lay within its spindly twigs, creating a concussive noise that echoed off the steep canyon walls, putting wrens and doves to flight. He didn't bother to look for the remains. He knew the snake load would have taken out anything lurking in the bush, removing head and hide.

Pappy holstered his pistol and resumed his trek toward his home, a cave high on the basaltic slope of a ridge. He'd found the cave some years past, too many years for him to accurately recollect. He wasn't a cerebral sort and since his arrival in the Superstition Mountains of Arizona and his good fortune in securing a relatively safe place to call home, he'd become less so, relying mainly on his senses to provide for his security. And greed. He knew the mine was there, somewhere. Despite the aging body that was forced to carry its burden, he had never given up the hunt. It occupied his dreams when sleeping, his thoughts when awake. And it had given him something else: an abiding paranoia. More than once he'd killed a human being who he felt was threatening his quest.

At seventy-one years of age, Pappy looked older. Deep rivulets creased his face. Ice-blue eyes had acquired a permanent squint against the harsh desert sun. His ears and nose had grown to outsized proportions and were festooned with long tendrils of hair. His mouth was a scabrous hole. A crushed gray felt hat, more fedora than cowboy, filthy with use and sweat, sat atop his head as protection from the sun.

Pappy had lived within the confines of the Superstitions for twenty-two years and emerged on infrequent but regular trips to Apache Junction to restock his larder with bags of beans and rice and flour and slabs of bacon, as well as seasonal vegetables and fruit. An aged mule named Jenny foraged patiently in a glade a half-mile from his cave, a spring that was Pappy's source of water. The mule was untethered and was content with its habitat. Occasionally, some greenhorn would attempt to capture the animal but Jenny was alert and quick and always managed to evade abduction. It knew it belonged to the grizzled old man who was generous with carrots and apples.

The mule named Jenny was Pappy's ride. On his trips for provisions he was astonished at the rapid growth overtaking the little town of Apache Junction. The 1949 film 'Lust for Gold' starring Glenn Ford and Ida Lupino put the town on the map. Once a truck stop across the barren reaches of Arizona sand with an all-night diner and not much else, RVs appeared, then permanent trailer parks. Soon, housing tracts occupied land once thought to be uninhabitable. Stores and shops sprung up, spurring further growth.

Now, when Pappy came to town, he was aware that he'd become something of a legend himself. He was likened to Jacob Waltz, the 'Dutchman.' He resented notoriety, fearing some greenhorn with an appetite for fame might try to dig up dirt on him.

Pappy's cave was covered with a large painter's tarpaulin more or less the same hue as the surrounding rocks, a grayish-black. At a distance, down in the cleft between two large ridges and looking up, it was difficult to make out the difference. At one time Pappy was able to scramble up the steep hillside but the ascent became slower with age. Now, he was in the habit of using his hands on top of his knees to assist with the climb, huffing and puffing his way up the hill. When he reached the right altitude there was a wide lip of rock that defined the entrance to his home. He warily pulled back an edge of the tarp and peered inside, letting his eyes grow accustomed to the darkness.

Pappy had had to fight for possession of the cave he called home. A mountain lion, bigger than the bobcats he'd seen roam the desert trails, had to be dispatched to earn Pappy squatter's rights. The wildcat immediately crouched down and snarled, revealing knife-like fangs, its wide-open mouth waiting to sink those daggers into warm flesh. The big cat was killed by a large-caliber bullet from Pappy's gun. He had chosen the Blackhawk because it was one of only a handful of handguns that could take down a grizzly. The cat's skin made an excellent blanket but despite all attempts to rid his cave of the reeking odor of cat piss, the scent persisted.

One of Pappy's first acts had been to lay out on paper the clues he'd amassed from reading the lore of the Lost Dutchman mine. He relied mainly on an account by Arizona newspaper reporter Sims Ely, who'd written the definitive history in a thin book published in 1956. It was after he'd set down the primary clues that he'd had an epiphany. Maybe he could persuade naïve greenhorns to purchase an interest in the mine. Hell, there were enough of them wandering around this wilderness, complaining about the heat and the total lack of civilization's comforts. They'd already been indoctrinated into the mine's history and they were here because they believed. If he could add to their excited prospect of becoming part of the history of the mine, they wouldn't leave the area totally bereft of anything to show for their trouble. They could be shareholders in the mine should it be discovered in their absence. When he'd put together rudimentary thoughts on how he should proceed, he did a little jig on the hard rock floor of the cave, giggling and carrying on, slapping his hat on his thigh in delight.

Pappy was a fugitive from justice. In Canton, Ohio, his previous place of residence, he'd been sentenced to twelve years in prison for forging signatures on government checks. As a postal worker in the USPS Cleveland Avenue office next to Malone University, he had ample opportunity to palm the checks. He knew the routine of the inspectors at their monitors watching the sorters do their work. He knew when breaks were taken and by whom, when brief intervals of distraction permitted him to pilfer social security payments. His undoing came when hotshots from Washington appeared with clever plans to determine the identity of the thief. This wasn't their first rodeo, and in short order Pappy was hauled before the magistrate who permitted Pappy to post bail pending appeal. Mistake.

Pappy's infrequent sojourns to Apache Junction were undertaken with a wariness usually reserved to animals seeking prey. He'd befriended only one person in the small town, Postmaster John Ains. He figured he'd soon be receiving checks from the greenhorns and it was essential that he allay any suspicions that might arouse an investigation. So, he told Ains what his intentions were and how he planned to do business.

After his latest foray to town, he arrived back at his cave and was on his third trip up the side of his mountain with a pack on his back of foodstuffs when he heard the shout.

"Come on back down here!"

Pappy turned, sudden fear bringing a surge of bile to his throat. Down on the flat, between the two ridges, was a deputy sheriff, his badge glinting in the late afternoon sunlight.

Pappy ditched the pack, scrambled back up to his hideout, pulled the tarp back and slid inside the cave. He panted from exertion and fear.

"Hey!" yelled the sheriff.

Pappy leaned toward the rock edge. "Come get me!"

There was silence for a few minutes. Pappy leaned back against the wall of his cave. He was thirsty. A moment later he heard the chinks of small rocks falling against the side of the mountain. His adversary was coming up the slope. Pappy gave out a snarl that sounded much like a cornered mountain lion. He stood and retrieved his .44 handgun and checked the chambers. Pulling down a box of soft-nose ammunition, he swapped out the snake load. The scrape of boots against the rocky scree sounded close.

"How'd you find me?" he yelled out the side of the cave.

"You're a fool, Whitlock! There's a picture of you on the wall of the post office."

"Ains ratted me out?"

"Was going to happen sooner or later, Whitlock. Now come on out of your hide."

Pappy answered by pointing the barrel of his weapon outside the tarp and pulling the trigger. The loud BOOM! of the .44 echoed off the canyon walls.

"Your aim is off, you idiot. If that's the way you want it, that's the way it's going to be."

Pappy ejected the spent bullet and replaced it with another one.

"Come get me!" he yelled.

There was nothing but silence. Pappy was breathing heavily. He knew he would never go to prison. He was too old, too set in his ways. Inside the cave, he felt trapped, powerless. With gun in hand, he pulled the tarp aside and stood on the narrow ledge that fronted the cave.

"Drop the hogleg, Whitlock."

Pappy hesitated, then holstered his weapon. The deputy had him right in his sights, his mean-looking automatic centered on his chest. It was a Kahr Desert Eagle in .50 caliber. The deadliest firearm in the world.

"What's the charge?"

The deputy, smallish at around five-seven or five-eight, wore a ranger's hat slanted down over his brows, dark aviator's glasses obscuring his eyes. His upper lip was hidden beneath a handlebar mustache in the style of Wyatt Earp. Without taking his eyes from Whitlock, the deputy turned his head and spat a stream of dark liquid.

"What's now, deputy? What's the charge?"

The deputy laughed without changing his aim. "The charge? You mean, before you took a shot at me? Maybe you didn't see your picture on the wall." He laughed again, then said with deadly seriousness, "Nice and easy. Drop the holster."

Pappy saw he had no choice. He unbuckled his holster and let it drop to the ground. The thought that dirt would sully the immaculate barrel made him cringe.

"You going to run me in?"

More laughter. "Run you in? Oh, hell no! You fired a shot at a peace officer. Know what that is? That's attempted murder!"

Pappy's eyes went wide. The man meant to kill him. "Wait on! You can't shoot me! I'm unarmed."

"Oh, no sir. We had a gun battle. Out here in the boonies, just like in the old days."

Pappy's mouth went dry. He began to tremble.

The deputy spoke. "Know what this here gun does to a man?"

Pappy knew. He thought he'd just dive down the hill. It would hurt like hell, but it'd be a damn sight better than being shot.

"This little .50 caliber baby is so dang powerful, you get shot anywhere on your body, your little left finger, you die from shock."

Pappy let his eyes drop to the side of the steep slope. That was a signal of sorts for deputy. That's when he took the shot. The bullet mushroomed when it hit Pappy's sternum, throwing him off the ledge and down the slope, tumbling head over heels, bouncing off rocks, finally landing on the hard desert floor.

The deputy watched, then fired three more shots. One was aimed at the canvas tarp, which blossomed inward. Another was fired at the rock wall abutting the cave, chipping off a large chunk of rock. The third shot was fired in a random direction near the cave. He emptied the shell casings and emptied them at his feet and holstered the Desert Eagle. Then he scaled the remaining distance to the cave and retrieved Whitlock's pistol. Using a plastic bag to mask his fingerprints, he fired five shots in a random pattern toward the slope where he'd been standing. Then he dropped the pistol. He threw the holster inside the cave.

The sounds of gunfire that had recently rent the peace of the Superstition Mountains were gone. The deputy rubbed his wrist. The tendons were tender, sore, from the massive recoil of the heavy weapons. He thought to himself how this would go down in the Maricopa County squad room. He played it out in his head.

"That old boy was mighty fierce. Drew his weapon and fired on me!"

"You put him down?"

"Had to! Didn't have no choice!"

He was a hero. A smile played on his face. His mustache twitched. A real-life gunfight! Maybe they'd make a movie about him. He laughed out loud.

In the Middle

Song lyrics by Phil Silverman

If you put your
Heart
In the middle
You can sing a better song
If you put your
Soul
In the middle
Then you know you can't go wrong
You know you can't go wrong
You know you can't go wrong

If you put a
Smile
In the middle
Happiness will be found
If you put
Love
In the middle
Your feet will lift off the ground
They lift off the ground
They lift off the ground

If you put
God
In the middle
You will sing a brighter song
If you put
The Lord
In the middle
You will know right from wrong
Will know right from wrong
Will know right from wrong

The Trip Over

By Michelle Cahill

Thirty-five days.
Sixty flying hours.
Thirteen thousand miles.
One-fourth the distance around the world.

World War II: These were the stats for Army Air Corp crews who traveled from America to airfields on the French island of Corsica in the Mediterranean Sea. My uncle, Lt. Tom Cahill, was one of these fliers.

My brother, my cousins and I never knew Tom—he was killed on a bombing mission near the end of the war. But I saw his picture in our home every day paired with a photo of his brother Jack, also killed in action. To us they were always unknown soldiers. Seventy years later exploring a box of old photos we stumbled upon over 500 pages of these uncles' letters home. I was shocked to see such treasures, having assumed all our family memorabilia was lost in a fire at my grandmother's house in 1964. As I read the letters, they begged me to compile them in a book. Tom and Jack brought themselves vibrantly to life—unknown soldiers no longer.

Though a bit esoteric for a child, whenever I saw their pictures I wondered if anyone besides our family cared that they had died. Once I met Tom and Jack through their letters, I became obsessed with military research and found their names in books and on documents and websites. I soon became connected with dozens of people including a few veterans who knew them and family members of other veterans they served with. History had taken good care of them. Indeed, they were remembered.

While I resurrected their past, it felt as if my uncles and my grandmother surrounded me. Cozy and spiritual are the best words to describe it. I wove my family back together, felt joyous, and never for a moment questioned if I was doing the right thing. Through the memoir I was compiling, these long silent voices would finally be heard.

Tom was in flight training for 18 months and wrote home often detailing how to fly a plane, land a plane, drop bombs and navigate pilots to specific destinations. In his last letter before leaving the States, he wrote to his mother about looking forward to seeing the world as he always wanted though he didn't yet know his combat location. "With any luck, I'll get lots of 'stick' time. After operational training here in South Carolina, I can now fly for fifteen minutes or so without making everybody in the ship sick from losing and gaining altitude."

In addition to the letters that introduced my uncles, other sources found me before I knew I needed them. For Tom, one of those unexpected connections happened when I met WWII veteran Sterling Ditchey who lives near me in California. *The Orange County Register* printed a story I submitted about finding the letters, the providential way I met my uncles. Sterling saw this story and was quick to email me. He, too, had been in the Army Air Corps, stationed on Corsica the same time as Tom but at a different airfield.

Sterling Ditchey, Bob Seur, William Morgan, Chuck Akius.

A week after meeting online, Sterling contacted me again to say he was looking at his shipping orders for the first leg of flying from the states to his combat location, an adventure affectionally known by all as the Trip Over. He and Tom with their crews shipped in the same formation in April 1944. Sterling was happy to reconnect with history, and it was exciting for me to see his scanned copy of these orders with his and Tom's names on the same page. Sterling subsequently found a second "original" of these orders which he sent to me to replace this same item of Tom's memorabilia that was lost in our family's fire.

Sterling's diary documented the crews' early departures from Savannah, Georgia, then West Palm Beach, Florida, where the ships and men received a traditional blessing by the Catholic post chaplain. All crews received these shipping orders in sealed envelopes, were given a compass heading southeast to Puerto Rico and told not to open the orders until they were airborne for one hour. Subsequently, Tom wrote two letters from Florida and nine headed vaguely "Somewhere in Brazil," "West Africa" and "North Africa." During Sterling's Trip Over, he kept detailed notes and flight logs. With this information, I identified Tom's likely same flight legs and landings, subject to adjustments due to weather, mechanical or airport issues. In addition to troop transportation, as co-pilot/navigators they ferried new twin-engine B-25s to their airfields.

Using Sterling's logs to recreate Tom's flights, landings in chronological order were at Georgetown, British Guyana; Sao Luis, Brazil; Natal, Brazil; and Ascension Island. Stops in Africa were Monrovia, Liberia; Dakar, Senegal; Marrakech, Morocco; and Algiers and Telergma, Algeria. Tom's crew then flew north from Telergma to Bizerte, Tunis, up the coast of Sardinia to Alesani Air Base, Corsica, France.

Sterling wrote about this once-in-a-lifetime experience which was full of excitement, hazards and splendor: "It was a long circuitous route, supported with only the most meager of radio and other navigational aids, one being half a clipboard. The flight depended almost entirely on dead reckoning navigation, that is, visual sighting of landmarks via computation of air speed, wind direction and speed, ground speed, and compass headings. No ground controllers monitored the flights, except on landings and takeoffs at the airstrips themselves.

One airfield where they landed had been recently hacked out of the jungle. It was a magnificent setting, doused by tropical rain every afternoon. Other airfields had obscured terrain and dangerously illogical landing approaches. Weather delays were lengthy. At one field, some ships received sabotaged oil, prompting emergency landings.

But there was also beauty. Of flying over the Amazon Jungle Sterling observed, "It was such a brilliant green that it looked as though there were floodlights shining up through the foliage."

En route from South America to Africa, the crews experienced 1,455 miles of the emptiest stretches of the South Atlantic Ocean. Sterling wrote, "This landless void of sky and water separates Natal, Brazil, and Ascension Island. Over these seas roll swift-gathering storms. In them abide schools of ravening sharks. We were aware of our chances of rescue if we were forced to ditch in these waters."

Sterling quoted *The Rime of the Ancient Mariner,* "Alone, alone, all, all alone, alone on a wide, wide sea." Of finally spotting Ascension Island, he wrote, "What a thrill to see the island, seemingly all of a sudden, rise out of the ocean after seven hours of flying over open sea."

Next came another one-day flight of 1,250 miles over water to Monrovia, Liberia, on the west coast of Africa. The following day's flight was a change of scenery from the vastness of water to the greenery of the lush coast to Dakar, Senegal.

Sterling's log continues, "En route to Marrakech from Dakar, over 1,000 miles of utter barrenness of the Western Sahara, we flew through a storm that at times was so violent that we were encountering sand at 11,000 feet flying altitude. We had an aircraft that was painted olive drab green, and the leading edges of our wings were sandblasted clean, down to the bright aluminum underneath."

At their next radio checkpoint, Tindouf, Algeria, they were cleared to Marrakech. The trick, though, was to get through the Atlas Mountains—they were too high to fly over. They had good maps and pretty good photographs, but there was only one pass—all other entrance canyons were dead ends. They flew up one, turned around, and found the right one the second try. Then it was easy from there to Marrakech.

"When we landed in Marrakech, we sure got our eyes  opened. We thought we were big stuff in our B-25 medium bombers, but on the field, landing just ahead of us were several squadrons of B-29 super bombers en route to India then Burma and China. They were *so big* that we could park our B-25s under their wings."

It had taken Sterling's crew 16 days to reach Marrakech. The B-29s had flown in overnight direct from Wichita, Kansas.

Though Sterling didn't know Tom, on Corsica they led parallel lives. Both were bombardier-navigators, primarily "bridge-busters" that warded off German troop and munitions movement into Italy and France.

Tom's last letter during his Trip Over was to his mother from North Africa, dated May 11. Both Tom and Sterling arrived on Corsica on May 12. Tom wrote his first letter from there on May 14, telling his mother he'd be stationed for a while on the stunning, picturesque island.

What Tom, pictured, didn't say that I learned from Sterling and other history resources was that within hours of their arrival, at 3:30 a.m. on May 13, the Luftwaffe made its final attack on the Mediterranean Theater, smack in the middle of Tom's bomb group.

Sterling's airbase wasn't hit, but he remembers being up most of that night, watching the fires at Tom's field north of his. Among the dead and injured were soldiers who had arrived with Tom and Sterling the day before. All received Purple Hearts, and those seriously wounded were sent home with total combat zone time of one day.

Without Sterling's help, I would have known only what Tom described in his letters—the people, food, entertainment—as he saw the world like he had hoped. I would have known nothing about the logistics of traveling there. By sharing his Trip Over, Sterling gave to me five weeks of Tom's life that I wouldn't otherwise have had. I will always be indebted to him for this.

Strong bonds form among those at war, and, interestingly, such was the case with Sterling and Tom who never met. My heart was deeply touched when after reading an early draft of my letters' compilation Sterling said, "I feel like I've known Tom all my life."

Mrs. Garner

By Jon Perkins

Warren Fielding took a vacation day to treat a neighbor to lunch. Mrs. Garner, an octogenarian with poor eyesight and pains too numerous to catalog, was fond of saying, 'I'm still standing!' to all who would listen, which weren't many.

Fielding was a bus driver for the unified school district. It didn't pay much, but it was gainful employment. He was stout and rapidly balding. His frail yellow hair had begun to ravel at the age of twenty-seven and had not abated in the ensuing ten years. In the meantime, his girth made up the difference, forcing him to amend his wardrobe annually at a cost that exceeded funds for entertainment. He had a large round face that was whiter than white and eyes colored a dun hazel that seemed to have been dredged from a slop bucket. He had never married and was resigned to his status as a single man.

The reason for the treat was his abashed discovery that the kindly Mrs. Garner, a widow of many years, had purchased a Visa gift card in the extravagant amount of one thousand dollars and had given it to him at Christmas. When Warren pressed her for an explanation, she had shrugged her emaciated shoulders and replied to the effect that her children were grown and financially secure and Mister Garner had left her a great deal of money.

"But why me?" Warren protested.

"Because, young man, you seem to be existing on a shoestring. You pay your rent and bills on time, and what you have left over, if any, you spend on necessities."

"That's fine, Mrs. Garner, I'm doing okay."

"Warren, it's not enough to do just okay. I would like you to do something you've always wanted to do. I want you to enjoy yourself."

That's when Warren suggested they have lunch together to talk about possibilities. He booked a reservation at the Four Seasons hotel dining room that had an expansive view of the Pacific Ocean.

The day was unremarkably sunny and warm, the usual fare for Orange County. The hostess noted their unease at being in the plush surroundings, he wearing a simple untucked green polo shirt over khakis and scuffed brown oxfords. Mrs. Garner had overdressed, wearing a pink silk dress that hung loosely over her wispy body, although her shoes were sturdy blue Skechers. They were shown to a fine table at the windows where they could enjoy the view. Warren remembered his manners and pulled Mrs. Garner's chair out for her.

At the waiter's suggestion, they ordered a glass of a French Viognier. Neither was a drinker, but this was a special occasion for the both of them.

"Oh, look at the lovely menu!" Mrs. Garner exclaimed. I know I would love a crab Louie. What about you, Warren?"

"I don't get out much," Warren ruminated while scanning the lunch entrees. He paused for a minute or so, then slammed the heavy folio shut. "Lamb chops!" he proclaimed. "I haven't had lamb chops since I don't know when!"

When the wine came and they clinked their glasses in a silent toast and took tentative sips, Warren thought he'd tackle the question of what to do with Mrs. Garner's endowment.

"I've been thinking," he started, "that maybe the best thing to do with the money is save it for a rainy day. I might have an emergency or something and it'll come in handy."

Mrs. Garner reached out and covered his beefy hand with hers, a withered and spotted appendage. "No!" she almost shouted. "That's not what that's for. I gave that to you so you could have some fun!"

Warren didn't know how to respond. 'Having fun' wasn't in his lexicon. He'd managed to survive by scrimping, making do with essentials, and not wasting money on bilious pursuits. His eyes scanned the tablecloth.

"What is the one thing you've always wanted to do, Warren?" she asked.

He looked up. "Fly."

"Fly?"

"I've always wanted to fly, to feel totally free."

148

Mrs. Garner laughed. She sat back in her chair, clutching her glass of wine, her eyes glittering in amusement. "Do you want to know something? I'm a pilot, Warren. I used to fly big bombers for the Air Force. I was a ferry pilot, taking the planes all over the country from the Boeing plant in Seattle."

"Really? What's it like, Mrs. Garner? To fly, I mean."

"It was mostly boring, except when an engine caught fire."

"Gee. I'm jealous."

Mrs. Garner chuckled. "I still fly, you know. When I can and my arthritis doesn't hurt so much. My license is still good, I've got a friendly flight surgeon who gives me a pass on my medical certificate."

"You fly? Still?"

Mrs. Garner was thrilled. It had been many years since she had received adulation from anyone. "Warren, that's what we'll do. We'll go flying. I'll show you the controls and you can take the yoke. My sight isn't very good, so you can be my eyes!"

A grin spread over Warren's face. When his lamb chops arrived, he wasn't so much interested in eating as in finding out more about flying. He quizzed Mrs. Garner about everything aeronautical and she answered in knowledgeable terms that weren't too esoteric.

"Warren, your food is getting cold!" She had almost finished picking at her salad, gleaning the crab from a surprisingly tall heap.

"Oh!" He picked up a knife and fork and cut a bite-sized piece of lamb. It hung on the tines of the fork but remained uneaten.

"When? When can we go, Mrs. Garner?"

"Well, for one thing, if we're going to be flying buddies, I think you should probably address me by my first name. It's Elizabeth. You can call me Liza if you wish."

"Liza! When can we go?"

"Oh, hold your pants on, young man. If you think I'm going to keel over tomorrow, you're wrong. I'll try to book a plane for some time next week."

"I didn't think that, Liza, you keeling over."

She chuckled. "I'm still standing, aren't I?"

The Balloon Man

By Doug Sainsbury

Directly west of Chicago is a boundary the city shares with the village of Oak Park, a community of approximately 55,000 residents. For 46 years into the 1980s, every Sunday afternoon in the spring and summer, Carmen Pistilli would drive to the intersection of Chicago and Oak Park avenues, unload materials from his trunk, and set up his balloon outdoor space from which he dispensed happiness.

He inflated a cluster of colorful balloons with his portable helium tank. Next, he fastened each inflated large balloon to a long, narrow dowel stick. Once all the balloons were ready, he would stand on the northwest corner of the intersection and proudly hold the cluster in the air. Motorists would stop and purchase a balloon or two for the kids; or was it more in gratitude to this old man who brightened children's eyes and provided parents with assurance, at least for an afternoon, that harmony existed in the world?

Mr. Pistilli, the son of an Italian immigrant, Angelo, a full-time balloon and novelty vendor, was raised in Oak Park and later moved to the northwest side of Chicago. Beginning in 1940, he worked as a machinist during the week and to remember his father, he sold balloons on this same corner on the weekends. A half-block to south on Oak Park avenue, the house in which Ernest Hemingway was born still stands, and three short blocks to the west is the Studio Home of Frank Lloyd Wright. Both of these icons lived in Oak Park for about twenty years; Hemingway from 1899–1918, and Wright from 1890–1909.

For the four-plus decades Mr. Pistilli sold his balloons on "his" corner, generations of Oak Parkers were born, raised, left the village as adults, and many, like me, moved back to raise their families. I attended church with my family a few blocks south of his corner and after the services, as we turned left at this intersection to head for our home in River Forest, we stopped at least once and bought these colorful treasures for the kids. Every Sunday afternoon as the light turned green, I guided the car onto Chicago Avenue as the kids would wave and marvel at the collection of vibrant balloons shimmering in the breeze.

If it was Sunday afternoon, Mr. Pistilli was on his corner and the planets were properly aligned. He was always there, every week. Years mushroomed fashioning decades. I'm sure if we looked closely, we would have noticed an increasing web of lines creeping across his face, but still, he was there, smiling. As one woman who grew up in the village recalled, "It was like he would never die."

Excerpt from a Future Novel – Joe's Story

By Sunshine Lutey

As the shadows grew in the cold November evening, I waited on our porch bench for my dad's return. In the dark I heard a car approach; finally, my dad was home! I saw red flashing lights. My heart raced as a police car stopped in our driveway.

The officer asked, "Are you Bob Peterson's son?" I nodded mutely.

"I'm sorry, son; there's been a car accident. Your Dad told me how to find you; I'll take to you the hospital."

I wasn't afraid for my dad; he could survive anything. With excitement, I climbed into the police car. The officer kindly explained how things worked. He even showed me how to turn on the siren, which I turned off quickly.

When he parked, I jumped out and raced into the building.

"Where's my father? I mean, where is Mr. Peterson."

The officer caught up with me and escorted me to the admission area.

A nurse approached; the look on her face scared me; she asked. "Are you Joe, Bob Peterson's son?" I was afraid to answer, but I nodded. She continued, "Your father is badly injured. He's in surgery; the surgeon is working desperately to save him."

My head felt light; the ground started to spin. I felt myself falling.

I found myself lying on a couch in the waiting area; a nurse asked. "Are you okay, son?"

She helped me sit up. I demanded, "I want to see my dad right now."

"But he's in surgery; you'll have to be patient. Joe, my name is Nancy; I'm from Social Services. Do you have relatives – an aunt or uncle, grandparent?"

I just shook my head.

She offered, "I'll wait with you." I nodded.

We waited three long hours; Nancy gave me some water and chips. Finally, a doctor walked directly towards us; his face looked tired, sad. "Son, I'm so very sorry; we weren't able to save your father." I didn't cry; I couldn't believe my invincible father was gone.

As Nancy patted my arm in an attempt to comfort me a women approached. Nancy introduced her, "Joe, this is Carol from Protective Services; she will help you. I have to go now."

Carol assured me, "Don't worry, we'll find someone to take care of you."

I knew I could care for myself; our bank accounts had enough money to cover expenses for a long time. I protested, "I don't need anyone to take care of me; I just need to get back home."

Carol firmly announced, "No Joe; you are not old enough to live by yourself; but we will help you; stay here while I complete some forms."

I needed this diversion; while she completed paperwork I slipped away and joined a family leaving the hospital; I crossed the parking lot and stayed far from the front door.

The day my father died I was almost taken into custody by the Michigan Child Protective Services; but that didn't happen.

A Change of Life
By B.D. Faw

My "Summer of '42" actually occurred in 1964. The few short weeks that I spent as a camp counselor in rural Virginia during that fateful, formative summer between my junior and senior years in high school can be targeted through the crystal-clear lens of retrospect as the pivotal point in my life. Many small events and circumstances, each insignificant in themselves, combined into the collective singularity, which ripped me from the black hole of my childhood and projected me--unprepared and overdue--into the expanding universe of my maturity.

When I arrived at the camp called Okie on the river named James, I was an insecure, awkward victim of puberty. The raging hormones of the prior year had stretched my thin frame eight inches, leaving the wardrobe of my mind in total disarray, with the dated fashions of a puny self-image strewn wildly among the poorly fitting trappings of a new giant. The runt in my mind--who now towered over his former tormentors--had no reference point from which to play their games. A "Stranger in a Strange Land," I turned inward for solace and may well have succeeded in total isolation, were it not for one old childhood friend who, through some still mysterious burst of perception and compassion, wrenched me from my safe haven within, and launched me irrevocably on a new course into the star-filled universe of life.

Al Welter and Camp Okie were a pair. Both were ancient, having served their masters well for over 30 years. Both had seen their usefulness absorbed for the greater benefit of others, and in the end, each was dismissed unceremoniously, with a few mumbled platitudes of gratitude, and then--on to the next generation. Al's retirement from the Marine Corps had come a few years earlier. Having devoted his youth to age-old traditions, he now dedicated his old age to instilling traditions in youth; giving to the Boy Scouts the devotion and leadership that his beloved Corps no longer found necessary.

The final days for Okie were still before me then. Strangely, (or so it now seems), I had no sense of import--no hint or premonition whatsoever--of the monumental changes that Okie's swan song was about to orchestrate in my life. I was just a lost soul named Bruce; cursed with a lispy, sibilance of speech; somewhat reminiscent of a grass snake--which made self-identification a living humility.

I came to teach. The only Sea Explorer at the camp, I taught knot-tying, navigation, and seamanship. My Navy whites served to distinguish me even more than my newly acquired height. A gawky scarecrow in a Popeye hat, I was immediately labelled "Sailor Bob" by the campers, whom we called "Grubs." Fortunately for me, it wasn't until several weeks later--long after I had permanently and irrevocably absorbed the name and attendant persona of "Bob" and had buried forever the waif who had been "Bruth"--that I finally discovered that Sailor Bob was the local clown who hosted the Popeye cartoons on Saturday mornings. What, a month earlier, would have been a devastating humiliation for the lost Bruce, was by then a source of wild hilarity for the emergent rogue now known as Bob.

Although, in retrospect, the transition must have come gradually during those fleeting, wild, and reckless days, I cannot recall a single moment of that summer that was not magic. It was as if Bruce had stuck to the upholstery of my father's car, and returned empty to the cold hostility of my new home in Arlington, Virginia--a home that I had not even finished moving into when I was whisked away to camp; a home that was by no means mine. I hope he found peace there, for I never saw him again.

In trying to pin down what I think of as the seminal moment--that instant in time which represents the birth of my soul--I keep coming back to the day when the first group of campers graduated. They had been at camp for two weeks, had worked hard for their merit badges, and even harder so that they could advance to their next stage of Scouthood. The crowning event was the awards bonfire, a formal scouting ceremony, held Saturday night to honor the achievements of these hard-working scouts. That bonfire was the terminal event of their camp experience, and parents often came to share the experience--peacock feathers out--strutting each other through our forest camp; reviewing their heir's accomplishments; brooding mothers quietly nesting together in the clean sanctuary of our linen-draped dining hall.

It was a family event, so along with the parents came eager younger brothers--in awe of the mysteries of wood lore; dreaming of taking their turns at these holy rites of passage--and bored teenage sisters who, resenting being hauled along to this childish event, assuaged their misery by dragging along a girlfriend or two. It was a small price for dad to pay to keep the peace and mollify dear young Lolita. For some reason (lost to oracles forever, I'm afraid), young girls tended to run in packs of three back then. Each covey had its queen, usually the sister of the resident grub.

Two certainties simultaneously coalesced from these conditions: Post-pubescent males--isolated from civilization in a military-style environment, and suddenly encountering the female of their species in full plumage and vulnerable to any diversion--suffer an immediate and devastating hormonal meltdown. Their drive to "score" is surpassed only by their total lack of any "cool" method of approaching their quarry. Any direct approach will spook the flock, leaving the hunter empty-handed, and the prey wary.

The other certainty, kept from our developing consciousness at the time by a mischievous Mother Nature, was that nothing in the world is more fascinating to a group of teenage girls cultivating boredom, than a group of older boys in uniform. And no uniform is sexier to them than a clean bright set of Navy whites. The sheer, simple, seemingly insignificant coincidence that only I had such a uniform was cause enough to forever divert the course of my life.

Sensing the attention of the approaching game, and desperate for an opening gambit, someone remarked "Hey! Sailors are supposed to be great with women. How about you going over there and collecting up some of those babes for us, Sailor Bob?"

I was immediately inundated with "Yeah, Sailor Bob!" "You can do it!" "We're counting on you!" and similar testosterone-triggered taunts. Trapped, with nowhere to go but forward--and my newly discovered persona hanging desperately in the balance--the fear of loss of status finally overcame the fear of failure, and I plunged forever over the precipice of daring.

Annihilating the black hole of my fear with the nebula of self-discovery, I strode forward, the bravado of inevitability rapidly replaced by the confidence of momentum. Approaching my probable destruction with a swaggering stride and a surprisingly easy smile, I took my cap and destiny in my hand and, with a sweeping bow, quipped "Hi, I'm Sailor Bob, your official camp guide, and I've come to show you around camp."

The universe continued. The sun still shone, but in mere seconds was surpassed forever by the radiance of three perfect smiles. The damsels were rescued from the dragon of tedium by a gangly white knight, reminiscent of Gary Cooper, and followed closely by a band of lesser knights--whom fate had cast instantly and forevermore as my followers. No longer would my self-image be allowed to embrace Lou Costello. I had loftier responsibilities to fulfill. The cosmic dust of my empty existence had reached critical mass, and a star was born.

The energy of that moment, and the momentum of maintaining my new existence, reached far beyond the remaining weeks of that summer--and the boundaries of a camp called Okie.

Returning to a home that had never been Home, integrating into a community I had not yet met--it was only natural to carry with me the only friend that I had ever been. Bruce never made it home. Bob replaced him in his first classes at the new school, and at the church fellowship group. Bob dated girls that Bruce had only dreamed of. He fell in love, had his heart broken, and recovered. He learned to live, and he learned to write. And perhaps most valuable of all, he learned that the only thing worth fearing in life is the fear of living it.

We ended that summer watching the flames kiss the clouds as they rose from the funeral pyre consuming what was left of the bones of our beloved camp Okie. We all felt a sense of loss: loss of the magnificent camp which had trained three generations of youthful leaders--gone now forever; loss of the constant companionship of new and often intense friendships, buffered only slightly by halfhearted promises to stay in touch, the impetus of which was already starting to erode even as the words hung fading in the dark; loss of our innocence, not sorely missed--but lost all the same.

But the universe is balanced. Each of these losses was offset by the many benefits that we all carried away with us: new knowledge, new confidence, new friendships, and a deeper and lasting awareness of self.

Amazingly, even as I watched the final flames of fraternity consume the last lingering log of our lives at Camp Okie, I had no clue--no sense of the apocalyptic metamorphosis which had just transformed my being. Galactic change is like that--subtle, gentle, hidden in the myriad events that make up our daily existence, but with the sheer, slow gravitational force to bend forever the course of our journey through life.

I had come to teach but had been taught. Now, the sweet, sad melancholy of nostalgia forever brushes my mind, and those magnificent, radiant youths, who shared my life and my birth, shall shine eternally from seats of honor around the ceremonial bonfires of my heart.

Freeway Highway

By Phil Silverman

K turns and turn around
Circles and u turns
Stay to the right to make your left
Or you will be burned and feel bereft-
Watch for those exits
In between SUV's
Proceed with caution
Replace anti-freeze;

I'm a driving man
From Cumberland-
County in New Jersey;
I joined EZ pass
Rather than plunk down 3 quarters
car insurance is high as a kite
Even under waters

The Three Comadres and Xochitl

by Peggy P Edwards

On July 7, 1987, María was in her last days of pregnancy, when she was shot in the back. The stray bullet came from the stolen gun of an angry gang member. Her boyfriend, Jose, rushed her to the hospital, bleeding and weaving in and out of life. She was taken to emergency care and he called Margarita, María's mother.

Margarita or Maggie called her two best friends Marilyn and Dorothy. The three best friends called themselves 'las Tres Comadres', or the three best friends forever. In a New York minute the three comadres met at the Mission Viejo hospital. There was nothing anybody could do. María died in Jose's arms just as their precious, perfect, beloved daughter was born.

María's last words were, "I want you to name my daughter Xochitl, precious little flower in Nahuatl. Take care of her as I would have. Jose, have Mom, Marilyn and Dorothy help you raise her. They will be her three *comadres.*"

And so María expired. Sadly Jose left the hospital, where Xo was to stay until released to the comadres, and headed for a bar. He was drunk when he climbed into his truck, put the pedal to the metal and raced off. He was stopped by the cops, shortly after released to the *migra* for being an 'illegal', having a criminal record and being a known gang member. He was deported and returned to his maternal home in Real del Monte, Hidalgo, México.

The three comadres' lives had changed radically. Of course they would keep and raise baby Xo, but first they had to re-arrange their lives.

Their friendship began twenty years earlier in southern California, after they met at a school function and discovered they had similar heritage south of the border. The three took pride in speaking, reading and writing flawlessly in both English and Spanish, and even a little French. They often spoke Spanish to each other, in order not to lose their fluency and so built a strong camaraderie.

The three friends enjoyed discussing their ability to raise perfect children. They each had two -- all of whom, except María, were either in college or practicing brilliant careers. The three comadres and scholars were respected and admired; they were senior teachers after all. Maggie was a science teacher and honored researcher; Marilyn taught literature and was a well-recognized Shakespearian; and Dorothy was the school's music teacher and, not to boast, the school's most popular teacher. Each excelled in her chosen field.

So the three grieving friends united after María's funeral and put together a detailed plan to do the best they could for their grand gift daughter. They would retire, buy a four-bedroom cottage by the sea, and design it to be the ideal learning environment for their precious baby Xo. Together they would raise the perfect child.

It didn't turn out to be that easy; the problems started from the beginning. They couldn't agree on the house to buy and finally, grudgingly, settled on one off Laguna Beach Coast Highway. Decorating became a hassle because each one thought their subject was superior and so wanted the most space and the best location. Maggie thought a science lab should be perfectly stocked and functional; Marilyn wanted every good book ever written in their library, from picture books to Shakespeare, Cervantes, García Márquez and Hemingway; Dorothy not only wanted the room with the most sea-sun light but also a piano, an organ and a myriad of other instruments. Serious arguments ensued.

But worst of all, the three of them were in love with baby Xo. They competed to make her smile, to hear her gurgle with delight, to hold her in their arms. They almost wouldn't let her sleep; one or more of them was always holding her or by her side.

As Xo matured, she began to realize she could get just about anything she wanted -- an angry look was sufficient, but if not, she would let out a blood-curdling yell and the three of them would immediately try to please her. She was being irredeemably spoiled. She did and said exactly what ever she felt like doing or saying, and not one of the three dared stop her for fear she would lose favor with their dear, darling baby Xo.

Not only that, the buying of toys, clothes and furniture for Xo verged on the absurd. When they ran out of baby things, they started buying things too mature for her. Discipline was out of the question. Not one of the three had the courage to stop or correct Xo. They were not raising the perfect child, they were raising a monster. They became Xo's obedient staff and actually a danger to her as well as to themselves, but they were blinded by what they thought was love.

The first warning was when, at the age of three, Xo climbed on the electric scooter they bought her and went flying down the street and into a wall at the edge of a cliff. She wasn't hurt too badly, but the doctor warned them about her safety and attitude.

Next she threw a tantrum so enormous that she broke a dozen toys and instruments because they wouldn't take her to Disneyland when she demanded to go. Finally, she was cruel and abusive to their little dog Saky and caused him to run away.

The three (hard to be friends anymore), were at their wits' end. They hadn't a clue what to do. They couldn't change their competitive ways, after all, that's what got them here, to this life of comfort. They couldn't stand being angry at Xo, and if they were, she changed that with a smile, which was irresistible. What to do? What to do?

Some good spirit must have been listening because one bright, sunny and on-the-edge-of-a-disaster day, José appeared at their doorstep. In his hand he carried an order from the judge demanding they turn over his child Xochitl — after all he was Xochitl's father by blood, as well as by birth certificate.

The three teachers, naturally, were heartbroken. They couldn't live without Xo. Their whole reason for being evaporated. Without Xo there was no purpose for their home, their way of life, and now they weren't even sure they liked each other. They even considered diving off a cliff into the great Pacific Ocean, a fitting end for their miserable failure as teachers and co-mothers. But as disasters tend to do, José's reappearance also united them again; the twenty-plus year bond could not be broken.

José, thankfully, had matured into a good and kind man and he saw the problem. He lost his way when he lost his parents when he decided to cross the border illegally into the U.S.A, but now they were together again and they taught him to be a good man. He invited his daughters' three saviors, las tres Comadres, to join him and his family in Real del Monte, México.

He said, "Sell your sea-side mansion and come and live with us. I'm sure Xo can hardly live without you. When she's alone with me she keeps asking me about you. We'll find something very rewarding for you to do, I promise."

The three comadres talked it over and decided it really was their only solution. In spite of all their problems they still wanted most of all to be together; actually, they couldn't think of anyone they'd rather be with – other than Xo. So they agreed – they would join Xo and José in México as soon as they could.

It didn't take long to sell their house; after all, it was in a prime location and they only asked a million and a half for it. After the last paper was signed, they gathered their children and reported their plan to move to Real del Monte, Mexico. Their children agreed that if this was what made them the happiest, then they must proceed.

So off they went, not with great illusions, but content to move to México to be near their Xo and with each other – grateful for second chances.

Once in Real del Monte they searched for the perfect place to call home for the rest of their lives. They discovered a lovely *hacienda* which the three of them found to be irresistible. Unfortunately, it was huge, it had 12 bedrooms, 6 bathrooms, an impressive living room, great kitchen, and super storage area, stupendous study and it looked over a magnificent valley. They agreed the sign to buy it were the little flowers that covered the valley at the foot of their mountain representing Xochitl, little Nahuatl flower. They were nearly 15 thousand feet above sea level and so they felt close to heaven.

But what were they going to spend the rest of their lives doing? Xo would spend time with them of course, but also with José and his family, and go to school. Besides, they didn't want to repeat their past mistakes with Xo – they now realized they had to give her space to grow.

Then Maggie had a brilliant idea. She noticed some seniors in town who seemed pretty neglected. They wore rags and were begging for food. What if they started a nursing home for seniors? Something new for them to do, if they could teach teenagers, caring for struggling seniors would be a piece of cake.

And so they did. The three *comadres* opened the first nursing home for seniors in Real del Monte. It turned out to be a necessity. The people were so appreciative they built a statue and a fountain to commemorate them. Xo joined them whenever she could and, as to be expected, she learned a great deal – after all, who could be wiser than seniors?

Xo grew up to be a model of goodness, kindness and intelligence. The Mexican people were so impressed by her work with their seniors that they elected her President of Mexico – after all, she was supported by centuries of wisdom.

Almost

By Sunshine Lutey

I have hearing aids
they almost help me hear.
I have eyeglasses
they almost help me read the newspaper.
I have a replaced knee
it almost lets me walk without pain.
I have a non-replaced knee
sometimes it's almost pain free.
I have a mind that does not remember names
almost all of the time.
I have a thoughtful husband
almost all of the time.
I have an organized home
almost never? Or almost some of the time.
These "Almosts" can be very disconcerting
almost all of the time.
Yet, I have an optimistic outlook
almost all of the time.

Airplane Mode

By Phil Silverman

Gave up nice aisle seat (from which to watch hips of stewardesses ....and easy access to restroom), so presumptive wife could sit next to presumptive husband. OK. I wind up in the middle seat – next to a 275-pound guy with butterscotch cologne and severe head-cold to my left, and little old lady singing "Jesus" songs to my right. (I think she muttered something about seeing Saint Francis, earlier, somewhere around Illinois.

On my way home from visiting my Brother in Irvine, California. Had a good week but that California sun is powerful. Need at least 70 sunscreen. Now back to Jersey.

No Santa Ana wind and low humidity; just bus exhaust and humidity upon which you could hang your winter coat.
But it's OK. I'm nearer my Blimpie Base in Holmdel and my Barnes and Noble haunt. What a Sports Section!

Back to the action -- sound of smooching. It's not from me or the lumberjack or the religious Twins fan, but coming from the three-seat row right in front of me. If you're going to talk me out of my cherished aisle seat at least keep your tongue in your mouth.

The hums, the swoons, the moans, the groans ...continued all the way to Newark. (It would have been OK if she was by herself). We hit two air pockets which only increased their joy!

All I had in my tum-tum was a full tube of potato chips and flat ginger ale. No more steak and eggs, pecan pie with cool whip, those miniature whiskey bottles, like in the '70s when I traveled to Pompano Beach, Florida. I'm weary, my undershirt sticking to my back, my underarm deodorant gel completely evaporated.
The stewardess gives me a nice smile ...C'est la vie!

We stop in Atlanta.

And what is this I see? The presumptive married or soon to be married couple stops at the bar concession at the airport. The bartender asks the dude, actually a real "Gentlemen's Quarterly" type, with a terrific jet-black coif, "a drink for your wife?"

He answers, "Well, we just started going out, ha ha."

Sooooo I went out of my way to enable some frat boy ...!!

Soon I'll be shuttled back to my bed. Curl up in a fetal position. No! I think I'll first stop at that nice Burger King at exit 116 or 117! A Whopper has my name on it! (I'm going with the Mayo this time).

No fetal position when I get back to my groovy garden apartment, either! I'll get determined! No more backing off when a girl says, "I'm very flattered but you see, I have a commitment ".

Once I watched a cool Robert Mitchum movie where he said, paraphrasing, "You can take anyone's girl as long as she's not married!" (Interestingly, I sweated through my Mitchum underarm gel on the Delta flight).

I'll call that girl before I even sit down for my nice decaf expresso! Well, tomorrow I'll return to the Eatontown Mall Cleaners with a bouquet for that manager, the black-haired, blue-eyed lady in the tightest possible jeans. If her boyfriend is hanging out there, I'll show him how to romance a girl!

No more giving up an aisle seat!

The Casserole

By Jerry Schur

Jason strode out the front door of the house first, and slid into his new red Porsche Boxster. While he waited for Robin to say her goodbyes, he pressed the starter button and nudged the gas pedal, smiling at the pulsing roar of the 350 horsepower engine.

Then Robin scurried out, holding her flowered, porcelain casserole dish, a treasured souvenir of their honeymoon in France ten years ago. The aroma of the leftovers she was taking home was still inviting. When she twisted into the black leather seat and swung her legs around, her skirt rode halfway up her thigh. After their first date Jason had told his dormmates that he'd just gone out with the most beautiful legs in America. Now he hardly noticed.

"I don't know why you bought such a small car," she said, shaking her head.

"I told you. It's my fortieth birthday present." He thought about his first car, a ten-year-old Honda. He had bought it when he graduated from high school with money saved from his job at McDonald's.

He roared out of the driveway and headed home. After a minute he said, "Great party."

"It was okay." She grimaced.

"That's all? Just okay?"

She shrugged her shoulders and said, "Nothing special."

He nodded his head. "Marlene always has such interesting guests," he said. "I thought this professor was fascinating. What was his name? Toplasky? Topolisky?"

"Close enough."

"Eastern religions are so interesting and he really knew his onions."

"All of a sudden you're interested in Eastern religions?" She turned to face him. " Why don't you get acquainted with American religions? We haven't been to church in I can't remember that far back."

"Hey, your casserole was a big hit. Delicious. What was it?"

"Do you really want to know?"

"Yes. I'm interested," he said without enthusiasm.

"Chicken Cassoulet à la Normandie. I got the recipe from a woman in my book club." Silence.

"Marlene throws such nice dinner parties," he said. "And the sunset from her patio on the hilltop was spectacular. You're lucky to have her for a best friend going back to your college days."

"I think she's changed since her divorce."

"How so?

She shrugged. He tapped the tape recorder button, and eight speakers stormed The Red Hot Chili Peppers into the car.

"Please," she said. She turned it off, and they rode in silence.

Until he said, "You're quiet tonight. Are you thinking about something?"

"No."

He asked, "Did I have too much Riesling?"

"You usually do, but tonight you knew exactly what you were doing."

"Score one for the home team," he smiled and marked a score in the air with his thumb. "You like the Borders. I thought Fred was very funny tonight."

"Yes, I usually like them, but tonight, just blah." She shrugged again.

"You're so quiet. Is something wrong?" He took his eyes off the road and glanced at her.

"No."

"Are you sure?"

"Yes, nothing."

He pulled into their garage. They got out of the car and faced each other, the car between them. He said, "You're as hard to please as the IRS."

"Yes, go ahead and insult me. You're Mr. Perfect. I'm wise to you." Her voice was shrill.

Then she smashed her casserole pot against the headlight of the Porsche. Ceramic and glass fragments flew. "You son of a bitch," she screamed. "I saw you hugging Marlene in the kitchen. I saw you kiss her." She staggered into the house, her shoulders heaving as she bawled uncontrollably.

Jason stared at the damage, shaking his head. Then he shrugged, smiled, and started whistling as he got back in the car. The tires of the Porsche screamed as he blasted out of the driveway.

It Is Not My Fault

By Sunshine Lutey

Several years ago, Sunshine's little sister Beth wrapped me, packed me in her suitcase and delivered me from Green Bay, Wisconsin to California. I know Sunshine really liked me; she managed to fit all her important items into me. I am a small, sparkling bright blue and green purse.

I'm a bit worn but we had three wonderful, exciting years together. I traveled with her wherever she roamed. Mostly I rode hanging from her shoulder or sat beside her in vehicles or at restaurants. I also enjoyed many shows that Sunshine organized.

In 2016, I went on a vacation with her and her husband, David, to a beach resort in Cancun, Mexico. It was beautiful there; often I sat with her in a balcony swing where we listened and watched the waves as they crashed on the shore.

She always had me tightly packed with her phone, credit, and ID cards, and everything else she needed. If she didn't remember to close my zipper, she could easily lose items. After a few losses, she thought about buying a larger purse, but she really liked me. Even as I grew old and worn, she chose to keep me.

It was a busy Friday -- she rehearsed at the piano with her husband and practiced songs with her CD player. I listened and

My owner, Sunshine and Tom Nash

knew she was ready. At 1 pm, she directed and performed the show at South County Adult Day Care Services.

After meeting and greeting audience members, she hurried to the Video Club to interview with Tom Nash for the Laguna Woods Stories, which is broadcast on television. Then in a yellow dress with a swirly skirt she danced at TGIF, a Village Club dance. Her friends, Mark Smith and Priscilla Preston, the Chordells, provided the dance music. While she danced, I listened to the melodious music and watched the dancers from a good vantage point under her chair.

After 45 minutes of wild dancing and twirling, she went home and greeted her husband David lovingly. Sunshine decided to carry fewer things in me; she dumped my contents on the table and selected a few items including her cell phone. With me slung over her shoulder, David and Sunshine drove to a Baby Boomers dance at Clubhouse 5 to listen to Phil Silverman perform. After she enjoyed Phil's renditions of five Elvis songs, they left. On the way out she opened me up because someone asked for her business card.

Back at home, she placed me on the table where I remained for another 36 hours.

Saturday morning, she sat down at the table and said "I'm going to put my purse back together again and put things where they belong.

"That's good," I thought, "I'm feeling very empty; things that used to snuggle up to me are missing."

One by one, she began to place items into my interior – business cards, credit cards, brush, checkbook, hearing aid batteries, etc. I noticed her face; frown lines creased her forehead in worry. Quietly she searched through the house for the little pink purse that contained the remote car key. She exclaimed aloud "It's got to be here; the car is locked outside in the driveway. I have not used the car since I returned from dancing Friday night." She searched endlessly.

Sunday afternoon, she finally gave up; "David, I've looked everywhere, but I cannot find the remote key for the Honda." David is a kind man but still doesn't like life's disruptions. He approached the problem logically and suggested places to search; however, none of the ideas worked.

On more than one occasion in the past as David watched her struggle to pack her needed belongings into me, I heard him suggest, "Sunshine, we should find a new purse that will hold your belongings easily and securely." Sunshine had ignored his suggestion. This time he more adamantly suggested, "Sunshine, we need to replace your purse."

Sunshine looked at me, her small, beautiful but damaged green and blue purse; she slowly agreed.

I tried to speak, but no one heard me; I said loud and clear, "It is not my fault."

We went shopping; she found a colorful larger purse with secure zippers. Everything she needed fit into organized zippered pockets and she seemed happy.

I was sad, but I was also happy for her and said, "My body is scraped and sore; I'm tired. I've served her well, but I guess it's time for me to retire. I had an exciting and fun life with Sunshine and David. I think her new purse will enjoy many wonderful events with her."

Tuesday morning, I was sitting on the kitchen counter waiting for Sunshine to place me in the recycle bin. The phone rang and Sunshine answered it. Her friend Judy had good news; "Sunshine, Clubhouse 5 called me. They found a pink purse; do you remember when I lost my Uke bag name tag? You put it in your pink purse to save it for me -- so they called me."

Sunshine walked over to me and patted my side, "It really wasn't your fault, you know; it was my fault. I must have packed my phone and the pink purse when I went to listen to Phil sing. As I left someone asked for my business card. When I extracted it, the pink purse must have fallen. I hope you understand why I need a more secure purse."

I'm glad she agreed with me and knows that I was right when I exclaimed, "It is not my fault!"

The Musician

By Peggy P Edwards

All life in Lalalandia was now dying or dead, except for Doremi Solati who wanted to live instead. Listen to her story and how she and her music saved the land of Lalalandia.

During these most terrible times people quit music good, bad and in between. They hated to love; they loved to hate more. They hated symphonies, operas and hip hop, cha-cha-cha, cumbia and rock. Dancing and singing were outlawed along with smiling, laughing and romancing.

The world was now broken; it seemed it could no longer be fixed. The land of Lalalandia was in a terrible jinx.

Doremi Solati was different though, she wouldn't and couldn't give up. She believed in the music that came from her soul. While the others used weapons – guns, knives and bombs; Doremi used music – strings, ukuleles and drums – clapping, tapping, whistling and singing always kept her from weeping.

Alas though her life was incredibly sad. She lived shut in with her family – windows closed, curtains drawn, doors locked – no fresh air was allowed, not at all.

The whole land and the town were all shut down. Hate took them over. It was over and done. No one was welcome, no, no one at all. Doremi's only real friend, Chris had packed up and gone – he hated the hate so had to leave town. But Chris was her partner, her soul mate, and playing music had joined them from a very young age. They both played the piano, guitar, ukulele and base. Their voices had power and range; they could sing anything anywhere with the music or not.

But the very lost people now hated the music; they could not stand it all. Whenever they heard it they would all yell in unison, "Turn off the damn music, stop that shrieking from hell."

They threw sticks and stones, breaking their windows, but aiming to destroy their homes and their bones. But Doremi Solati could not and would not stop it; it comforted her soul. She did quiet down but did not and would not stop. Sadly, she thought, she would soon be through with this life once and for all. She considered just leaving, but where would she go? The whole world was ruined; there was no place to go.

An old woman and her old man in the middle of town tried to remember the good ole times but what for? They could see and feel the cruelty of the land going bad. They lay in their bed in each other's arms, listening to the end of their weak thumping hearts. They heard the zinging of bullets and blood-curdling yelling. The sun was no longer shining. It was dark all around.

Now was the time, it's now or nevermore. Thought Doremi Solati. *What's the point of all this hiding if it's over and done, or is it?*

She picked up her ukulele and walked out of her door. She ran right to the middle of town. She started to sing, her voice was heard far and wide, except by deafened terrorists, too dumb and too full of hate to hear a beautiful song.

But the ones who could hear her dropped their guns, knives and bombs. The music was entrancing and so were the songs. The old woman and her man started laughing, dancing and romancing, and soon, so was the town.

Just then, up waltzed Chris harmonizing with her lovely song, *Always*.

But also, just then, one of the haters threw a stone that hit Doremi Solati in the middle of her forehead. But, no need to worry for her soul was filled with music and she could nevermore be stopped.

The haters started yelling, "Cover your ears, don't listen to this music from hell." But the people kept on listening and now you could hear them saying. "Wow, I love the sweet music, I think I'll sing along." The music made them feel good, a feeling they had almost forgotten, but now newly sprung.

The people started singing, dancing, laughing, and even crying (like they never had done). You could hear "I like you" and "I love you" all over town.

Always became Lalalandia's anthem and they sang it whenever evil entered their town, or any time they felt down. Doremi Solati was their hero, and the monument built in her honor said, "Doremi Solati was the hero who saved our Lalalandia with her music and her song we will *Always* remember." And that's all.

Whose Dog Are You?

By Annie O'Hara

One day I awoke and lying out by my curb,
Was a mangy old mutt, with a sign—"Don't Disturb!"
"Whose dog are you? Are you mine?" I requested.
But he looked at me, growled, then loudly protested.
"I could not possibly belong to you.
Now leave me alone, or I'll chew on your shoe!"
"How about Mrs. Jones, who lives down the street?
Could you be hers? She seems rather sweet."
"I would not belong to her, because she has a cat.
And this dog detests them, so let that be that."
"How about Mr. Greely, who works with my Dad?"
"Never. You see, he lives alone and that would be bad.
When he's at work I'd have nothing to eat.
There'd be no one to call me if I ran in the street."
"How about Maggie, she goes to my school?"
"Surely you're kidding, that girl is too cruel.
She likes to tie cans to little dogs' tails.
Then she bellows in laughter, it just never fails."
"Well then, I'll ask you again and don't be a jerk.
Will you come live with me? You know it would work.
So, whose dog are you? Could you be mine?"
"I guess that I could, yes, that would be fine."

In memory of Annie O'Hara.
She loved all of our dogs in the village!

The Authors

Jill Amadio

Jill is from Cornwall, UK. She has authored and ghostwritten memoirs and a crime series. She wrote the bestselling World War II biography of a fighter ace, and co-authored a Rudy Vallee memoir. She ghostwrote an autobiography for a former Laguna Woods resident, retired U.S. Ambassador William Hussey. Jill was a reporter in London, UK, for the Bangkok Post, Thailand, and the Spanish-American Courier, Spain. In the U.S. she was an investigative reporter for Gannett Newspapers. She narrates audiobooks and had a role in the movie, "Dr. Zhivago." Her crime series is set on Balboa Island, Orange County, California.

Michelle Cahill

After 40 happy years working at Disneyland, California native Michelle's first year of retirement launched her publishing career. Her initial book is a compilation of recently discovered letters to her grandmother from two uncles who died in World War II. *Dear Mom: A Family Finds Its Past in World War II Letters Home* reads like a novel but every word is true. Her second book, *Tail Wags and Purrs: Happy Pet Adoption Stories,* recounts uplifting tales from her 20 years' experience helping abandoned pets find loving homes through animal shelters and rescues groups. Both books are available on Amazon.

Professor Alan Dale Dickinson

Alan is a native of the great state of California. He was born in downtown LA (Los Angeles). And, he has written and published ten mystery/suspense novellas in twelve countries. Alan is also a retired Vice President and Business Banking Manager, World Corporate Lending Group, from Bank of America. He has a BA in Business Administration-Finance with a concentration in accounting, economics, real estate and management. He holds a Lifetime Community College Teaching Credential from the State of California.

Peggy P Edwards

Peggy was born and raised in Mexico City and came to the United States to complete her education. She received her BA from Southern Methodist University and her MA from the University of Wisconsin. She taught university, college, ESL, high school, elementary, and preschool—always focusing on Spanish and English. She is now retired at Laguna Woods Village. She is President of the Publishing Club. She published *Alfabeto Crossover Alphabet* and *Lalalandia*— eight bilingual, mystical, magical stories of a land saved by music that you'll want to read about.

Margaret Estrada

Margaret was born and raised in Stockton, California, and graduated from University of Pacific with an Elementary Teaching credential. She taught school in Stockton, married and raised four children. She also attended Seminary and is a Diaconal Minister in the Methodist Church, where she teaches adult classes. In her second marriage, Margaret sailed in Mexico with her husband Dan on a boat he built named "Spirit". She has 8 grandchildren and a great granddaughter. She enjoys watercolor painting, weaving, and writing her stories.

B.D. Faw

Bob Faw is a multifaceted Renaissance man: writer, prize-winning poet, editor, publisher, actor, director, songwriter, teacher, engineer, entrepreneur, radio and television host and producer. His stories, essays, articles, and poems have been published in books, magazines, newspapers, the Internet, and a freeway Time Capsule. His poetry collection, Cycles of Love is published by The Abstract Press. Bob

179

is a Vietnam veteran Marine with degrees in Mathematics & Computer Science (UNT) & Interdisciplinary Studies (Masters-CSUSB). He founded, built, and sold three technology companies before teaching mathematics, computer literacy, & video production at King Middle School. He moved to The Village in 2003.

Daphne Fineman

I was named by my brother, Stanley, after Daphne du Maurier, who also enjoyed writing and wrote historical facts for the Studios. I was born in 1936. As a child living in London during World War II, I was evacuated to the countryside, where I spent many happy years, in spite of the threat of invasion, I would hear and tell many stories, to keep myself amused. I never thought about writing a book until I was 81 years old. I have lived a very full and interesting life; I was eighteen when I left England for America after a broken love affair.

William Scott Galasso

Scott is the author of sixteen books of poetry including *Mixed Bag,* (A Travelogue in Four Forms) (2018) and Rough Cut: Thirty Years of Senryu (2019) available on Amazon. In addition, he edited *Eclipse Moon*, (2017), the 20th Anniversary issue of Southern California Haiku Study Group.

Dennis Glauber

Dennis is a retired anesthesiologist originally from South Africa and a longtime Seattle resident, now of Laguna Woods Village. His writing expertise has included the writing of program notes for Music of Remembrance in Seattle, The Seattle Chamber Players, and now for the Community Concerts of Laguna Woods Village. His essays have appeared in *The Hummingbird Review* and in various journals in the Pacific Northwest. He is an active participant in the Spoken Word Club, and his stories have been featured at the Publishing

Club's annual storytelling events since 2014. He was a prize winner in the Village Library's writing contest in 2013.

Lorraine Gow

Lorraine Gow is a black immigrant (*legal*) from a "banana republic" still working through all that entails. Lorraine was educated by Hungarian nuns with a side order of Jesuits: "I am forever trying to make peaceful compromises—some positive, others mired in mud." Her writings reflect the compromises which are the cobblestones that have paved the road of her travels, dreams and anxieties. Her writings have appeared in the *Village Stories* anthologies 2015-2018, *Lummox Poetry* and *Life and Legends Literary Journal.* She is currently working on a collection of short stories and one of poems.

Larry G. Johnston

Born in St. Louis, Missouri. Larry became a Navy Submarine Torpedoman in San Diego. He graduated from the LAPD, Police Academy. Larry was a Policeman in Newport Beach and the City of Orange. He holds a B.S degree in Psychology and Law from S/E Missouri State University. Larry retired from the Orange Co. Marshal's Dept. as a Lieutenant. He has written his *Autobiography,* a mystery *Mammoth Highway's Big Pine Murder*, a *One Liners* old sayings book and a children's book, *Spanky Is Adopted* about mini donkeys. Three of his books are available on Amazon.

Jacqueline Jorgensen

Jacqueline was born in the hills of Puerto Rico. "School is not for girls" her parents claimed - bad news for Jacqueline who wanted to learn to read and write. Life was a living hell, working on the farm all day, then sent to other jobs. When she was twelve years old, she ran away from her miserable home. She got married and later divorced, and moved to California. At age thirty-two she entered a Junior College, after which she began writing about her turbulent childhood and all the work she did to learn to read and write. She has published three books.

Dorothy Kuhr

Dorothy has been an artist all of her life, and able to express all of her emotions and creativity through her art. The poem that Bob Faw wrote for her on her birthday has inspired her to create in words the emotions and feelings that in the past she could only express through art.

Sunshine Lutey

Sunshine, from Wisconsin, moved to California with her husband, Lloyd Lutey, in 1962. During 43 years of marriage, they raised two children, Darrell and Denise. She earned a BA in psychology/sociology from San Jose State University and worked as a programmer/ designer of business systems. This year she celebrated 10 years of marriage to David Hartman. Sunshine loves to write and performs/directs musical shows; see her music, articles and activities at SunshineCharities.com. *Village Stories* 2015-2018 include some of Sunshine's articles. Sunshine is very thankful to the Publishing Club for providing the opportunity and knowledge to become a published writer.

Lydia Mascarin

I was born in Los Angeles, California. Since childhood I have had a passion for nature and art. I have sculpted, painted, and written poetry. When I came to Laguna Woods Village I sang with the Kool Kats. I am now writing short stories and Haiku.

Ellyn Maybe

A Southern California based poet and United States Artist nominee 2012, Ellyn has performed both nationally and internationally as a solo artist and with her band. Her work has been included in many anthologies and she is the author of numerous books. She also has a critically acclaimed poetry/music album, *Rodeo for the Sheepish* (Hen House Studios). In addition to her band, her latest poetry/music project is called ellyn & robbie. Their album, *Skywriting with Glitter* has also received high praise. For more info about Ellyn and her projects, go to https://store.cdbaby.com/cd/ellynrobbie2 and ellynmaybe.net.

Miranda McPhee

Miranda grew up in London, England, and had a career in the financial services industry. Between work and play, she has visited thirty countries, both big and small. She lived in Paris for five years, came to the US in 1999, and has lived on both East and West Coasts. She co-authors *WiKIDly Awesome Travels*, a series of activity books for young globetrotters, two of which have won a Family Choice Award (www.wikidly.com). She is also responsible for the publicity for the Old Pros of Laguna Woods theater group (ocoldpros.org), which keeps her pretty busy.

Annie O'Hara

Annie O'Hara; poet, actress, editor, publisher. She created 'The Missile', a huge success during her exciting career in Aerospace with TRW/Northrup Grumman. Her heartwarming poetry book 'Poems Everyone Will Enjoy' brings laughter and tears and may be purchased on Amazon. Her latest poem. 'Whose Dog Are You?' was written in memory of 'Dolly' her Dalmatian. May all dog lovers enjoy!

Mi Ja Park

Born in North Korea and moved to South Korea shortly after the Independence of Korea from Japan in 1945. She came to the USA through the Exchange Visitor Program and became a Registered Nurse. Later, she became interested in teaching. She graduated from the University of Arkansas with a BA & M.Ed. majoring in Special Education. She is a lifetime member of National Education Association. After retiring from teaching, she and her husband, Ok Park, moved to Laguna Woods. She founded the Gotchiga group which is composed of Korean single ladies in Laguna Woods. With a newly found interest, she enjoys writing for fun.

Jon Perkins

Jon harbored a passion for writing that was realized when he left the corporate world. Since then he has written fifteen novels and a bunch of short stories. *Emerald Cove*, *Crystal Cove*, and *Diver's Cove* are a series of beach-read novels. *Hammer*, *Quayle*, *Gunny*, and *Derek* feature protagonist Jack Hammer, a Marine who finds trouble wherever he goes. *High Treason* was published in 2017. *Armed Conflict, Golden Grace* and *Snake Trail Peak* are three unpublished thrillers featuring a wife and mother having a Concealed Carry Permit.

Daneen Pysz

Daneen has written many songs and stories about women in the Bible. She portrays and tells these women's stories in first person dramas. Each piece was researched by Daneen, using the Bible as the primary reference and using various other sources, but most of all, she was guided by the gift of the Holy Spirit. She performs her stories for congregations, retreats, fundraiser and can be reached at: daneen.pysz@gmail.com. Her book, "Bible's 'Bad' Girls…the lesser known brave and courageous women of the Bible" can be purchased on Amazon.

Allan Rankin

Allan has lived in Laguna Woods since 2017. He moved to California in 1962 and continued his career in the telecommunications industry. *Phone Man–A Memoir* was published in 2017. One of the articles submitted in *Village Stories* 2019, is a book review written many years ago for an English class while studying at Saddleback College. *Landline,* is a byproduct of being a phone man for 50 years, and just intended to lighten your day; and *A Tree Grows in Brooklyn* is a book long forgotten by most people, but worth revisiting.

Douglas F. Sainsbury

Doug was born and raised in Chicago's west suburbs of Oak Park and River Forest, Illinois. Education included OPRF High, School Hemingway's alma mater; University of Illinois - BA English; Juris Doctor from IIT's Kent Law School. U.S. Army, including fourteen months in Vietnam. Forty years in the banking industries, the last nine years with the Federal Reserve Bank of Chicago. Doug retired to Southern California in 2011 to be closer to his children and to pursue his lifelong dream of writing fiction. His novels include *Intrusion, Phantasm*, and *Emergence.* Doug can be contacted at dougsainsbury@gmail.com.

Joan Arlene Schumm

Joan is a writing consultant, speaker, and author of *The Top 10 Traits of Silicon Valley Dynamos.* She is published under the name Joan Clout-Kruse. Her articles have been published in newspapers, journals, and the Internet. Born in San Francisco, Joan wrote professionally for corporate America and Silicon Valley from 1960 to 1995, including Ampex Corporation, Stanford University, UC Berkeley, Nikon Research Corporation, Charles Black and Shirley Temple Black. She has lived in Laguna Woods since 2010.

Jerry Schur

Jerry graduated from the University of Wisconsin, Madison and then went to Yale Law School. He then practiced law in Chicago for forty-eight years, hunting with the big dogs, i.e. litigating against the U.S. Government and some of the biggest corporations and insurance companies. After years as a snowbird he moved to Laguna Woods in 2014, where he was delighted to discover Saddleback's creative writing courses. Jerry has contributed to *Village Stories* since 2016.

Daya Shankar-Fischer

Daya is a native of India who lives in Laguna Hills. She came to America in 1960 to further her education. She earned her graduate degrees MA and Ph.D. in Philosophy and Global Communication from Ohio University, OH. Prior to retiring in California, Daya was a professor at the University of Northern Iowa. IA. Her teaching profession offered her the opportunity to travel to many countries across Europe, South America, and Asia, and to Russia. She has published articles, stories in journals, and activity books for classrooms. She supports the Educational Foundation of the Native Americans and the children's school in South Dakota Pine Ridge Reservation.

Cheryl Silverman

I was born in Detroit, Michigan, and moved to California in 2011. I am still caregiving in Orange County, but especially since marrying Phil in 2018, I have developed an interest in photography and poetry. Phil has been a great mentor in the latter.

Phil Silverman

I'm a transplanted Jersey Boy. I grew up watching the Manhattan skyline and attending Yankee ballgames. Moved to CA in 2009 after 30 years of New Jersey State service and 12 years of public service radio on WBJB-FM. I have thrived in The Theatre Guild, Sunshine Performance Company and the Publishing Club. For the PC, I enthusiastically contributed some poetry and a short play.

Suellen Zima

I grew up reading and writing. At the age of 40, in 1983, I emigrated to Israel. A fascinating visit to China in 1988 set me on a nomadic path, teaching in several parts of Asia and returning often to a constantly changing China. I published my first book, *Memoirs of a Middle-aged Hummingbird*, in 2006. The twists of life made my second book, *Out of Step: A Diary To My Dead Son* come to life in 2013. I have loved filling my website and blog (www.zimatravels.com) in the last 20 years in Southern California.